The Adventures of
BURT ALVORD

BOBBY BROWN

ISBN: 978-1-66784-638-5 (printed)

ISBN: 978-1-66784-639-2 (eBook)

DEDICATION

This book is dedicated to my grandfather:

Rodney "Pabo" Alvord

TABLE OF CONTENTS

INTRODUCTION

This fictional novel is based on the true life of Burt Alvord, a lawman who turned outlaw, train robber, and fugitive in the Old West. Credit for inspiration for came from the well-written biography: *The Odyssey of Burt Alvord* by Don Chaput. Burt Alvord is considered my real-life cousin and what makes his story all the more interesting is that one of his gang members shared the same name as mine – Bob Brown. My grandfather, Rodney Alvord has a very similar build and face structure to Burt, not to mention they are both left-handed. George Parsons, whom you will meet later, is a relative on my wife's side of the family. George lived in Tombstone the same time as Burt and his family. Though George was older than Burt, undoubtedly, they both would have come across one another at some point. George was good friends with Wyatt Earp and his brothers, and witness to the gunfight at the O.K. Corral in 1881. George chronicled his life on a daily basis in Tombstone as can be read in: *The Private Journal of George Whitwell Parsons* edited by Carl Chafin, which provides interesting insight into what it was like to live in the Old West.

Though it might be exaggerated, it is believed that as a teen, Burt witnessed the gunfight with evidence that Burt worked at the O.K. Corral at around the same time. I believe this is where Burt and George would have met as the O.K. Corral was the center for departures and arrivals. Later in life, Burt was appointed to Cochise County Deputy Sherriff at the young age of twenty. Over his years serving as a lawman, he gained a tough guy reputation, and many people agreed with the methods he used to keep their town safe. However, Burt frequented many saloons, and gained the reputation of being an alcoholic. Supposedly, Burt met and associated with many outlaws in these saloons that influenced Burt's desire to get rich by way of robbery.

Burt turned in his badge and formed a gang with Billy Stiles, Bravo Juan Yoas, brothers George and Louis Owens, Bill Downing, Bob Brown, and "Three Fingered Jack" Dunlop. The gang caused havoc in the region by robbing trains, cattle rustling, and armed robberies. One of the gang's most well-documented events was the attempted Fairbank Train Robbery, which ended in disaster when they were stopped by Jeff Milton. Burt then escaped from prison more than once as he and his gang continued their robbing spree in the West. Though Burt and his gang's reign was short, their true story deserves attention, a Hollywood Blockbuster in the making. Little is known about Burt Alvord after 1906, but it is believed that he left for Central America, specifically to the Panama Canal where he lived the rest of his life.

1: TOMBSTONE GUNFIGHT

6:00 AM

Burt Alvord tossed and turned in his bed like most nights in Tombstone, Arizona. Reoccurring dreams of a man falling off a horse, himself playing pool, participating in gunfights, train robberies, and escaping prison flashed consecutively underneath his eyelids. The most disturbing of the visions was a man pointing a gun and shooting Burt. He could never make out the face of the man, but the same series of events occurred in his dreams on most nights.

Burt's heavy breathing and low murmuring woke his father, Charles, who got out of bed and peered into his son's room. Charles shook his head when he saw that his son was sweating again. Charles slowly crept inside Burt's room, avoiding the loose floorboards so as not to startle the boy. As Charles stood watching his son, he could not help but believe the night terrors would be the end of his son one day. He reached over to the bedside table and grabbed a dry cloth to pat Burt's forehead.

"Wake up son, you were dreaming again," said Charles.

Burt opened one eye and saw the concern in his father's face.

"Any new details this time?" Charles asked.

Burt took a sip of water before answering, "Yes, a new ending. I was overlooking water with a woman standing next to me."

"Interesting, well, you best be waking up soon anyhow to get ready for work, I have to head to the courthouse again this morning," said Charles.

Charles walked away as if this was routine. He was a very important man in Tombstone being the town's Justice of the Peace. He sat in grand jury and civil cases daily, along with arresting citizens who violated the law. He did this at least a few times a week. It was Wednesday, October 26, 1881. That morning, he left at the same time as his son Burt, but they headed in opposite directions. Charles in the direction of the courthouse as Burt strolled to the O.K. Corral.

The grueling desert sun rose and was shining bright like most days at the O.K. Corral. Tiny dust devils blew across the stables as the horses rested on the ground in the shade. Owner of the O.K. Corral, "Honest John" Montgomery was meticulous and kept a watchful eye on his proud livery making sure the horses were well taken care of while he kept his accounting books in order. Fourteen-year-old Burt Alvord was his most trusted and reliable of the employed stable boys. Day after day he worked hard brushing the horses, shoveling their feces, and preparing the horses for rent which was usually for a trip to Tucson. Not a day went by when Burt didn't assist lawmen, outlaws, and cowboys on their future journeys. As long as Mr. Montgomery got paid, he didn't care who hired his horses. Burt worked in the O.K. Corral with his energetic friend, ten-year-old Billy Stiles whose job was to keep the horses fed and hydrated. During their breaks, Burt liked to read and write, while Billy liked to nap.

10:30 AM

Burt was busy brushing a horse when he heard a loud neigh on the other side of the corral. It seemed like a horse might be in distress. Billy, who was napping in a haystack, awoke suddenly to the sound of the commotion. Both Burt and Billy looked over to see what was happening. The man on top of the horse struggled as the horse repeatedly kicked its front legs up and down. The man was no match for the horse and he was flung backward to the ground. Burt watched the man fall as if in slow motion. He couldn't believe what he was seeing. The man who was thrown from the horse was the same one Burt kept dreaming about. Burt, Billy, and the others rushed to aid the man and calm the horse. Burt reached him first.

"Seems to be unconscious," said Burt out loud.

The man was clean shaven but wore round spectacles which had broken in half. Burt's eyes were drawn to a reflection emanating from the man's silver belt buckle that read *Panama*. Burt was then pushed out of the way by his boss, Mr. Montgomery who lifted the man up from under his arms and dragged him toward his office out of the sun.

"You boys go on and take a break, I got this," said Mr. Montgomery.

Billy smiled knowing he could go back to sleep and extend his break. Both Burt and Billy walked over to the haystack and rested their eyes before continuing their work.

Fifteen minutes later, it was about noon when Burt opened his eyes. He was unable to sleep due to Billy's snores, which were too loud for anyone to fall asleep around. Burt then began doodling on a piece a paper he'd pulled from his pant pocket. Deciding he had enough of Billy's snorting he nudged Billy, waking him up. He handed him his scribbles and asked, "Here, tell me what this says?"

my name is Burt Alvord.

Billy opened his eyes, examined it, turned his head to the side and frowned, "Egyptian hieroglyphics?"

Burt laughed, "No, no. This is called mirror writing." Burt handed him a small mirror and showed him what the image was through the mirror.

"Oh! How strange. I see it now, it says: *My name is Burt Alvord*," said Billy.

Just then Mr. Montgomery yelled from across the way, "Break is over, back to work."

People came in and out of the O.K. Corral all day, and business was good. Burt prepared the saddles, as Billy refilled the water buckets for the horses.

2:55 PM

A man ran into the O.K. Corral, sliding on the dirt before stopping himself. He enthusiastically yelled, "A gunfight is about to take place by C.S. Fly's Photography Gallery!"

Burt and Billy looked at one another, dropped what they were doing and ran to see the action.

They came upon other Tombstone citizens observing the scene. When they got closer to the crowd, they saw five men facing four other men arguing at one another, all with their hands ready at their holsters. Burt immediately recognized the men, as all of them had passed through the O.K. Corral more than once. The group of four men consisted of brothers Virgil, Morgan, and Wyatt Earp, along with Doc Holliday. On the other side, the five men were Tom and Frank McLaury, Billy and Ike Clanton, and Billy Claiborne.

"Hey Billy, look that's my friend, Frank McLaury, he's the one who taught me how to shoot. And look over there, that's the famous Wyatt Earp," said Burt.

3:00 PM

The church bell could be heard in the distance indicating it was the top of the hour. The two sides continued to stare each other down. The tension between the men could be felt as it reverberated through the onlookers including Burt and Billy who ran for cover in case of an ensuing gunfight. They hid behind the Photography Gallery's wall but still had a visual on the nine men.

In an instant, guns started firing, and men fell to the ground wounded. With all the commotion Burt and Billy ducked down hoping no stray bullets would come their way. After thirty or so seconds, the guns were silent. The two boys poked their heads up to see the damage. Only one man was standing unharmed, Wyatt Earp. Both his brothers Virgil and Morgan, along with Doc Holliday were wounded but alive. Wyatt kept his gun at the ready surveying his surroundings. Burt noticed Frank and Tom McLaury, and Billy Clanton on the ground not moving. Burt's eyes specifically went to Frank, whose head was bleeding.

"No! That's my friend," Burt yelled and started running toward Frank as other townspeople came out from their hiding places to see what had happened.

"Don't go over there, are you crazy?" Billy called.

Burt ignored him and stood looking down at his lifeless friend. Next to Frank was his gun on the ground. Burt dropped to his knees and put his hands on his forehead as his emotions turned to anger and he looked over to Wyatt Earp. Burt turned back toward Frank and picked up his gun. He stood slowly, heart beating so rapidly he could hear each bump, but before he got the chance to point it at Wyatt Earp, Billy grabbed his wrist and whispered fiercely, "Think about what you are doing. If you shoot him, they'll hang you for sure."

Burt looked at Frank, then back at Wyatt. Speaking to Billy he said, "One day I'll be in charge, and no one will stop me from protecting my friends." Burt then placed the gun under his waistband for safekeeping. Just then, Burt's eyes were drawn upon a woman who had her arms around Doc Holliday. She was tall with dark hair, and her beauty froze Burt in his stance.

"Snap out of it, Burt," said Billy.

The woman noticed Burt staring at her. He awkwardly looked away, and then he and Billy left the scene to finish the rest of their day at the O.K. Corral.

5:00 PM

Later that evening, Burt went into town in hopes of hearing more about the gunfight. He walked into the popular watering hole, the Crystal Palace. Inside, Burt had never seen the place so busy. Everyone was talking about the gunfight with mixed feelings. Some said Wyatt Earp, his brothers, and Doc Holliday were heroes, while others called them murderers. Burt had never experienced such energy from his town. But Burt soon grew bored of hearing all the drama and needed to focus his energy on something else. His ears heard the loud smack of billiard balls on the far end of the room. There were three tables in total, with two crowded. The other had only two men and they looked to be soon finished. He approached that table and quickly realized the two men were twice his age. He was reluctant to speak at first, but found the courage after realizing they both were bad players.

"I'll play the winner," Burt interrupted.

The two men ignored him and continued with their game.

"I said, I'll play the winner," Burt said again.

"Beat it kid," said one of the men.

Burt grabbed a billiard stick, broke it in half over his knee and reached back to swing it at the man. As the stick came forward, the stick was stopped in midair by a hand. His eyes followed the hand, which became an arm, then a shoulder, and to his surprise it was the face of a girl with long blonde hair. He looked into her deep blue eyes and was immediately taken aback.

"Best you control that temper, you wouldn't want to get hurt," she said.

Burt's face grew red, embarrassed. He let go of the stick, swallowed his pride, and walked away. The two older men were unfazed and laughed before continuing their game. *That's the second time I've been stopped today,* Burt thought. Then someone was tapping his shoulder. He turned to see the girl had caught up with him now standing outside the Crystal Palace.

"Sorry about that but there has been enough fighting for the day," she said.

"Well, I don't need protecting miss …," he paused struck by her eyes once more. "What's your name anyway?"

"Lola," she smiled.

"Well, uh …," he stuttered, "I best be going; I hope to see you again."

Lola blushed and smiled, and then they both went their separate ways. After a few steps, Burt turned to stare at Lola walking back into the Crystal Palace. He thought to himself, *One day I'll marry that one.*

2: GEORGE PARSONS

It was July 1885, and four years had passed since the gunfight, yet it was still a common discussion in town. Burt, now eighteen years old, continued to work at the O.K. Corral alongside his now fourteen-year-old friend Billy. He visited Lola as much as possible preferring to meet at the Crystal Palace where they engaged in deep conversations about life and the future. Lola once wondered where Burt got his crazy ideas until she learned of Burt's love for reading. Though Burt did not have much of an education he loved diving into a good book. Reading allowed him to expand his imagination, as well as provided inspiration for becoming a lawman.

Burt was a frequent customer to Tombstone's first library: *Parsons Books*, but the story of how he became a frequent customer was comical. The library was owned by George Parsons. Burt saw George on occasion at the O.K. Corral, but it was not until George saw Burt reading a book at work that he first approached him.

"Like to read kid?" asked George. "You should come down to my new library tomorrow for its grand opening."

"Sure thing!" Burt answered enthusiastically.

The next day Burt walked into the library. He immediately noticed a musty smell. Though the odor was strong, it gave him comfort. The library was small but the shelves were filled with row after row of books. George met Burt at the front door and asked, "What do you like to read?"

"I fancy adventure-type books," he answered.

"Ah! I have just the one for you. Have you read *The Adventures of Tom Sawyer*?" George pulled the book off one of the shelves.

Burt's eyes narrowed, "Five times at least!"

George put the book away and pulled out another holding it up high, "Yes, but did you know there is a sequel – the *Adventures of Huckleberry Finn*."

Burt's eyes lit up and he started at the front cover, "No idea there was another Mark Twain book." He happily took the book from George and quickly flipped through the pages. "How much to rent?" asked Burt.

George looked outside and saw a man approaching the front door but then answered with a smile, "Well kid, being that you are my first customer consider this a free gift to rent, but in exchange I need you to help paint the outside of this building. If you agree, I need the book back in good condition when you're done."

Burt paused to think, and believed he was being played knowing the story of Tom Sawyer all too well. "Hey! I know what you're getting at! You won't pull a fast one on me," he proclaimed with a stern look.

George laughed out loud, "Good catch! Thought I had you there for a minute."

"Look! My father is the Justice of the Peace, and he wouldn't take too kindly to your jokes."

"Oh Burt, it was only a joke: we readers need to have a sense of humor you know."

Before Burt could answer, a man entered the building. Burt was surprised and recognized him by his long dark mustache, it was Wyatt Earp. Wyatt paused to take in the shelves of books before speaking to George.

"It's been almost three years since I've seen you, old friend. How are you?"

George put his hand on Wyatt's shoulder and seemed happy to see him, "Has it been that long? What brings you to town?"

Burt was not a part of the conversation and wasn't sure if he should leave or stay. He held his book and turned to leave but spotted another book on a shelf near the door. It was titled: *Frankenstein.* He had heard of the book from his father but never had the chance to read it. He looked to see if George or Wyatt were paying attention, they weren't. He grabbed the book quietly, hid it under his shirt and took two steps outside before hearing Wyatt commanded, "Stop!"

Burt stopped dead in his tracks, and his face grew red as he slowly turned. He immediately knew he was in trouble and tried to think of a good excuse.

"Take it out kid," Wyatt said.

Burt looked down in embarrassment not finding the excuse fast enough. He slowly uncovered the book and mumbled, "Was only borrowing it."

"You don't want to go down the road of a thief kid, it never ends well," Wyatt advised.

Burt's face remained red, but he suddenly felt a surge of anger toward Wyatt, "You're responsible for killing my friend Frank McLaury. Why would I listen to you?"

"You don't understand the whole situation kid. I am sorry that it happened," Wyatt responded.

Concerned, George interrupted hoping to put an end to the conversation. "Kid, I cannot let this act go unpunished. Seems to me you will be painting the library after all."

Burt held his head up; handed George the *Frankenstein* book, then folded his arms defiantly, "What? No way!"

"Unless you want your old man finding out," said George.

Burt's eyes opened wide at the thought. "Fine," he agreed. "When do I start?"

"Tomorrow morning and every morning after that until it's done."

"I have no time. I work at the O.K. Corral," pleaded Burt.

"You best wake up earlier then," said George.

Burt shook his head and frowned before storming off, still holding the *Adventures of Huckleberry Finn* book. Wyatt and George watched Burt as he walked away.

"Kid has a lot of maturing to do," said Wyatt.

"Maybe you should teach him how to throw a baseball; looks as strong as an ox. So, what brings you back here?"

"I'm actually here to see some old friends like you. Things have been going well in Idaho, but now my wife and I are looking into moving to San Diego. The real estate market is booming, and we want to buy up some saloons and gambling halls there. We need a trusted friend to help run them. Would you be interested?"

"Oh! Wyatt, you certainly bounce around a lot. I appreciate the offer, but I have my heart set on moving to Los Angeles one day. Perhaps, one day, I could help run your businesses."

Wyatt smiled, "So be it, old friend. Have a drink with me tonight. Kate is also in town."

For the next several days, Burt honored George's request and showed up in the early morning and painted the outside of the library. He figured that the short punishment would allow him to read more books from the library in the future. However, on the eighth day of painting he woke up at the usual time to go paint, but he was tired. He hadn't slept much the night before. More night terrors led him to sleep on and off throughout the night. *I have to find a way to get someone else to do the painting*, he thought. It was an unusually brisk morning, which just added to the fact that Burt wanted to go back to sleep. He showed up at the library as expected to continue working. Just as he started, he remembered the scene in the *Adventures of Tom Sawyer* when Tom persuaded the other children to do his work by making them trade small treasures with him for the privilege of doing the painting. "Reverse psychology," he said out loud. Just then, off in the distance, he noticed his friend Billy who was clearly on his way to work at the O.K. Corral.

"Hey Billy, come over here!" he yelled. Burt then pulled out the *Adventures of Huckleberry Finn*. He had finished reading it the day before and planned on returning it to George.

"Need something Burt?" his friend asked.

"What I have in my hand here is the best book, I have not read it yet, but hear it is full of adventure. I will let you borrow it when I'm done," said Burt.

"Sure thing, thanks, Burt," said Billy.

"I can't let you borrow it that easy though," he said in an under-handed tone. "You see, I'm having so much fun painting this here library that I wish I had time to read it. The sooner I get done the sooner I can let you borrow it," he explained.

"No problem! I can paint it for you, I have a little time before going to the O.K. Corral," Billy offered.

Burt's eyes lit up, he couldn't believe that it actually worked. Billy grabbed the paintbrush and continued painting the library while Burt sat off to the side with the book opened. From Billy's perspective, it looked like Burt was reading but instead, he was sleeping. Not soon after, George came upon the scene. He knew exactly what Burt was doing and decided to put an end to it quickly. He lightly kicked the bottom of Burt's shoe waking him up. Burt opened his eyes staring at George's boots and knew who it was at the sight of them. He slowly looked up at George who had an expression of contempt and a cigarette dangling from his mouth.

Burt stood up slowly, exuding guilt. He told Billy he'd finish up, and would see him later.

George scanned Burt's face seeing the exhaustion. George could relate, "I know how you feel, my home is infested with fleas. Sleep is impossible."

Burt handed George his finished book and started walking over to the paint can. Instead of making Burt finish, George stopped him.

"You're almost done with the whole thing, let me finish and you go off to work," George offered.

"I never leave a job unfinished," said Burt as he started to paint.

"A great quality to have," said George. "You are welcome to finish, but I want to give you some advice. Your mind is your greatest weapon. When doing anything you ought to think of a plan before doing it." He then looked over at Billy who was now off in the distance, "Lastly, be good to your friends and they won't backstab you in the future."

Burt nodded hearing every word. Not much later, he completed the job with his last brushstroke of paint on the library. George patted him on the back giving a vote of confidence that he had learned from his mistake. George then pulled out the *Frankenstein* book and handed it to the shocked Burt.

"I want it back in a week," he said with a wink.

For the next two years, Burt frequented George's library where he would borrow books free of charge in exchange for conversation. In 1887, however, George moved to Los Angeles and took all the books with him. These two years not only allowed Burt to gain a friend, but an advantage over many other people, and that advantage was knowledge. Burt had little time to dwell on George's departure as he had been recruited as the Deputy of Cochise County not long after George's departure.

3: RECRUITED

Burt was sitting inside the Big Cage Theatre, a small theatre filled with around thirty wooden chairs, a handful of tables, all facing the stage. Musical and theatrical shows occurred on a monthly basis from acts that traveled through the country. Bullet holes littered the walls, and the smell of beer and smoke always engulfed the room. Burt sat with his now wife Lola, waiting for a musical act to perform. He saw her often but soon his time with her would be limited. It was July 15th, 1877, the day that changed the course of Burt's life. On that ominous day, Sheriff John Slaughter walked into the theatre looking for Burt.

John was an older man with gray hair and a matching gray goatee. He was hard-nosed from spending many years as a Texas Ranger, and fighting for the Confederates in the Civil War. He favored his shotgun which he never let out of his sight. He tapped Burt on the shoulder and asked if he could have a word. John had already spoken to Burt over the last couple weeks about recruiting him to be his deputy with the blessing of Burt's father. Burt was well built at this point in his life and much stronger than the average man. He had a reputation in Tombstone and Cochise County as being well tempered and unselfish, yet not a person willing to back down from a fight. John liked those characteristics in Burt; however, he quickly realized that Burt also liked to frequent the saloons to drink. Despite this, he felt there were good things to come from Burt, and he wanted to put him to the test.

"We need to leave now," he said quietly.

"Can't we just wait until after the show? I am with my wife."

"Deputies don't wait for shows to end when there is a job to do. Being a deputy means considerable travel," said John.

"You mean I am a deputy?" asked Burt.

"Temporarily deputized Burt. You will get paid for this, but you must show me you got what it takes if you want to do this full time."

Burt rolled his eyes, huffed, and grabbed his prized Frank McLaury gun. He then gave Lola a kiss on the cheek and left with John. Outside, two horses were strapped to a wagon. They were heavily equipped with supplies of food and gun ammunition for a long journey.

"We're going to go pick up Juan Lopez who is being held in jail, north of here in Solomonville. He murdered a man last year, and we've been tasked to take him to Willcox."

Both men rode the wagon to Solomonville – it was about a three-day ride. Once there, they took the prisoner to Willcox for another three-day ride. Burt soon realized the work was gruelingly long, as they trekked through the heat of the desert. However, it was work, and he knew if he showed well to the Sheriff, he would hire him again in the future. Sheriff John and Deputy Burt did not speak much to Juan Lopez during the trip other than asking him if he was hungry. Once in Willcox, the handcuffed Juan was taken to get a bite to eat at the local saloon. John tasked Burt with keeping an eye on the prisoner while he went to the jail to meet up with Sherriff Scott White to do the paperwork before Juan could be let in.

"I am going to get a drink at the bar while you eat," Burt told Juan.

For the next hour Burt drank heavily as if it was water and he was lost in the desert. Juan took the opportunity to slide his chair over to the next table and started talking to some rugged-looking men. Burt didn't notice and just focused on drinking. Not soon after, Sheriff John walked into the saloon and spotted Juan speaking with the men and saw Burt at the bar. Sheriff John watched the men Juan was talking to and feared they were discussing an escape plan. Sheriff John then noticed Juan doing something odd with his hands and quickly realized that he was working a hand loose from the handcuffs. Just as Juan was about to break loose completely, Sheriff John barreled over and stuck his shotgun in Juan's gut ending any plot to free himself. Burt was now drunk at the bar and was soon confronted by Sheriff John.

"First rule of being a lawman is not letting the prisoner out of your sight," the Sheriff said sternly.

"Sorry John ... *hiccup* ... I only had my back turned for a second," replied Burt.

"Don't let this happen again," demanded John.

They dropped Juan off at the Willcox Jail and moved on to their next task. Sherriff Scott White had informed them that there had just been a deadly train robbery in Sonora headed by Jack Taylor and his gang. Jack Taylor was caught, but his gang had gone into hiding near the Whetstone Mountains in Cochise County. Sheriff Scott agreed to lend his deputy Cesario Lucero if they were willing to pursue the gang. Before Sheriff John could say anything, Burt eagerly agreed for the both of them. While Sheriff John was about to give up on Burt, he saw a fire in his eyes. *Perhaps he just wants to see more action,* John thought. He appreciated Burt's enthusiasm and agreed to the manhunt. The next day, they left with the wagon pulled by the same two horses, as Cesario rode next to them on his own horse. The trip was only a day's ride, and it was not long till they could see the mountains in the distance, but the sun was starting to go down.

"I know those mountains well; they're not too far out from Tombstone. My best guess is that they're on the east side since there's less sun in the afternoon," said Burt.

Just then Cesario saw something moving in the distance. "Look there," he pointed.

"Looks to be a man riding toward those mountains," said Sheriff John.

"Well, let's follow him," said Burt.

They slowly headed in the same direction as the man and watched as he disappeared around a peak. By that time, the sun had set and the crickets were starting to chirp. The men continued though hoping to find some sign of the man or the gang. They slowly made the turn around the same peak and suddenly came to an abrupt halt. There was a campfire not far away with a handful of men resting around it who appeared oblivious to the noise of the creeking wagon. Sheriff John, Burt and Cesario hoped off the wagon and crept in close to the men by foot. Before they could get any closer Sheriff John pulled Burt and Cesario in close.

"Alright, this is the plan. We need to take them fast and fierce. They won't expect it. Guns drawn, let me do the talking," Sheriff John ordered.

"Shouldn't we wait for them to fall asleep, that would give us more of an element of surprise?" suggested Burt.

"I'm in charge, don't question me," Sheriff John snapped quietly.

Burt nodded but inside he didn't agree. The three men walked slowly toward the campfire, guns at the ready. Burt held his trusted Frank McLaury gun, Sheriff John with his shotgun, and Cesario with his Winchester rifle. They soon noticed there were only three men lying next to the campfire looking like they were about to fall asleep.

"Hands up!" demanded Sheriff John.

The three men were startled leaping to their feet.

"Who's there?" asked one of them.

"Sherriff John Slaughter. Are you men a part of the Jack Taylor gang?" he asked.

The three men stayed where they were and looked at each other not answering. Burt watched as one of the men reached slowly underneath into his bag and pulled out a gun. Without hesitation Burt began firing on the man. A firefight ensued as they all started shooting at one another. Burt, John, and Cesario quickly backed away to find cover behind some boulders. Within seconds, they realized only one man was now firing at them and the other two were on the ground. Seeing his friends had been wounded, the man realized he was outnumbered, and it was not long before he threw down his gun and put his hands up. Burt was first to emerge from behind the boulders and handcuffed the man. John and Cesario helped the other two men up who were bleeding, one from his left side, and the other man from his shoulder. They quickly escorted the three men, all in handcuffs, to the wagon.

"State your names!" demanded Sheriff John.

The man with the shoulder wound answered for all of them, "I am Francisco Nieves. This is Guadalupe Robles and Juan Soto."

Guadalupe was the man shot that had been shot in his side. He was bleeding heavily and soon fell to his side. Burt checked his pulse and said, "He's dead." Sheriff John did not have time for sympathy though. They could have easily been the ones dead. "Burt, Cesario, we're heading out. Let's take these men to the Tombstone jail."

They took Francisco, Juan, and the now dead Guadalupe to Tombstone without stopping during the night. Burt kept an eye on the men inside the wagon while Sheriff John controlled the horses. Cesario continued to ride his horse but did not stay with them. Sheriff John directed him to head back to Willcox and tell Sherriff Scott White of the capture.

"You're shot, are you okay?" Burt asked Francisco.

"Call me Nieves, and yes I'm good, clean shot straight through," he said. "You know you can make more money being an outlaw," Nieves added.

Burt could see the sincerity in his eyes and said, "You can also get shot dead. Why make the sacrifice?"

"I had a regular job once, ran my own restaurant. You will meet plenty of outlaws doing what you're doing, but they will all have the same story," said Nieves.

"Hush now. Burt, stop talking to them. They will fill your head with nonsense," Sheriff John said.

They kept quiet for the rest of the ride to Tombstone but Burt would never forget the conversation. They dropped the men off and placed them inside Tombstone's jail completing their job. Sheriff John was satisfied, paid Burt a few dollars and told him he did well, and that he would be contacting him again for future jobs. Eventually, a few months later, John, directed Burt in early November 1887 to move to Willcox and work with Sherriff Scott White as he needed him in the area for more manpower. Though he moved to Willcox, he traveled throughout Cochise County doing various lawman jobs and visited Lola whenever an opportunity presented itself. He planned to marry her when he had a more stable career.

4: LIQUOR CELLAR

"**N**o, no, stop! No," Burt was dreaming again. He sat up quickly in a deep sweat.

"Again, huh?" Lola asked. She got up out of bed, grabbed a wet towel and placed it against her husband's forehead. "Fifteen years since I met you and never once have you talked in detail about these dreams. Why?"

Burt searched for his flask at his bedside table, grabbed it, and took a quick swig of whiskey. He closed his eyes ignoring the question and went back to sleep for a few more hours before he had to wake up to go to work.

Burt and Lola had married in 1897. Burt had become a well-seasoned lawman at this point in his life. He acted as deputy for nearly a decade before he was recently hired on as Constable of Willcox by Sheriff Scott White, which meant he would not have to travel as much. He was now the head law officer of a town of five hundred people filled with various saloons, hotels, and merchants. The town was an important stop on the Southern Pacific Railroad and filled with promise as a great region for raising cattle. The nearby larger towns of Pearce and Dos Cabezas didn't even have a railroad. Willcox, however, was ruled by wild and wooly cowboys. Burt vowed to put his foot down and make some real changes.

Like most days, Burt was not well rested. On that day, November 10th, 1897, Burt started his day by going into town for a drink and bite to eat at Kasper Hauser's Saloon where he would meet up with one his deputies and longtime friend, Billy Stiles. Burt entered the saloon wearing black boots, tan denim pants, a white shirt with a brown vest fixed with his Silver Star badge, and a round brown hat. He saw Billy and went to sit with him.

Kasper hurried over to the Constable with Burt's beer, already familiar with what he wanted because of his regular occurrences.

"Thank you, Kasper," Burt said as Kasper sat his drink down.

Burt gulped a quarter of his beer before he turned to Billy, "Say, we need another deputy around here, who do you trust?"

"There's only one man in this town other than you who I would trust my life with, that's Bob Brown," said Billy.

"Great – tell him we need him and the pay will be good," Burt responded.

Some noise could be heard from across the bar. Two men were being loud, and arguing with Kasper. "Get out!" Kasper yelled.

Burt took one more sip of beer before standing to address the situation. The two men now had their hands on their holsters but were stumbling around and slurring their words. Burt confidently stood behind the two men, grabbed them both by their neck collars, and threw them outside. Billy smiled as he watched. "I'm eating breakfast!" Burt yelled. "Sober up and stay out of my sight."

"Thank you, constable," said Kasper.

Burt tipped his hat and nodded before sitting back down with Billy to finish his breakfast. "Now Billy, go get Bob Brown, this town is starting to get reckless."

Later that evening at Burt's office, he received word that the Erie Cattle Company had just loaded some train cars with cattle and there were two men causing problems and threatening to kill the cattle. Billy and now Bob who had been successfully recruited stood in the office awaiting directions from Burt.

"I task you Billy with taking Bob with you to investigate. You have my permission to shoot on scene if warranted," said Burt.

Bob and Billy hopped onto their horses and raced to the location. Burt stayed behind and instead of waiting decided to go across the street to Kasper Hauser's Saloon. It was nearly dark. A handful of people were there drinking, playing cards, and shooting pool. Kasper quickly filled up a beer glass, and delivered it to Burt as he sat down at the same table from that morning. Burt took a sip of his beer and looked to his right and noticed a man shooting pool by himself but his form was all wrong. He was a younger man, most likely in his teens. Burt got out of his chair, beer in hand and walked up to the pool table.

"Anyone ever teach you to play before?" Burt asked. The combination of Burt's low voice and his big build seemed to intimate the man, not to mention the Silver Star on his vest. "No sir Constable," the man replied.

Burt set his beer on the ground, then grabbed the pool stick from the man and said, "Well your form is all off. Here, grab that end of the pool cue with your right hand, and that end between the fingers of your left hand." Burt pretended to hit the white ball to show him. He then continued, "And bend your knees slightly, it will help you with balance."

Burt made sure the pool balls were in their correct place ready to break before adjusting the white ball. He pulled the cue back slightly, and with much force he shot the white ball at the pool balls causing them to scatter across the table. Only one ball went in, the number nine-striped ball. "You see, that ball went in, now I am stripes, and you are solids. If either of us hit the 8-ball in before knocking in all of our balls, then that person loses. Understand?" Burt asked.

"Yes, sir, Constable," the man replied.

Burt shot his number fourteen ball in, then the eleven, followed by the thirteen. "See with a little practice, you can do this too," Burt said. He then narrowly made the number fifteen ball as it ricocheted off the number 8-ball. *Slam* – suddenly there was a loud noise at the entrance. Burt turned around quickly with the pool cue still in his hand. It was the same two men who had caused problems that morning. They were drunk and laughing with their hands on their knees trying to catch their breath at the same time. Immediately, Billy and Bob entered with their guns drawn on the two men who were still laughing.

All the patrons quickly got up and ran out the door, including Kasper not wanting to fall victim to any stray bullets. Burt kept his eyes on the men as he stepped forward, but he kicked over his beer causing it to spill, resulting in him slipping and falling to the floor hitting his head. The pool cue slammed to the ground with a loud crack. Billy and Bob stared at Burt who was knocked out cold. With no hesitation the two men punched Billy and Bob in their guts and grabbed their guns from their hands. Billy and Bob had no choice but to put their hands in the air.

"Think about what you two are doing. What are your names?" asked Billy, hoping by talking to them the tension would ease.

"I am Andy Darnell and this is Billy King. We don't think, we just do. It's what makes us such good outlaws," said Andy.

"You two sound like the dumbest outlaws I've ever met," said Bob.

Burt came to, and felt the back of his head as he laid there on the ground. He grimaced as he sat up and tried to make sense of the situation in front of him. His eyes focused for just a moment but he was still dizzy. "Unbelievable," said Burt.

"All right you three, down in the liquor cellar you go," Andy ordered with a wave of the gun he held.

"Move it!" yelled Billy King, keeping his gun drawn on Billy and Bob, escorting them downstairs as Andy walked over to Burt and took the gun out of his holster, the same gun that once belonged to Frank McLaury. Andy grabbed Burt under the arm and forcibly helped him up. "Off you go!" Andy yelled.

Burt stumbled as he grabbed the back of his head. He made his way slowly down the stairs to the liquor cellar with Andy pointing the gun at his back. Andy locked the door and ran back upstairs.

Bob looked out of the small window with crossbars up toward the stairs. He grasped his hands around the crossbars and shook it violently. Neither the door, nor the cross bars moved, they were locked in for good. Meanwhile, upstairs, the men were having fun.

"Yeehaw!" Andy yelled.

"I can't believe that worked," said Billy King.

For much of the night Burt, Billy, and Bob could hear the two men upstairs throwing glass bottles, yelling, and playing pool. The three of them sat on the ground, Burt leaned up against a beer keg, as Billy leaned against the wall, and Bob sat on an empty crate that he had flipped around.

"What do we do, Burt?" Billy asked.

"Nothing we can do. We can't get out until someone lets us out," Burt replied. He then opened up a lid on one of the barrels, cupped his hands in the beer, and drank.

"Ain't no one ever escaped from prison?" Bob asked.

Burt and Billy gave him a funny look.

Bob continued, "Look, in my past I may have had a few run-ins with the law, been to prison once or twice. I can assure you we can escape this small cellar."

"Go on," said Burt.

"It's called the art of deception. We need to make them think that we got out. Therefore, we need to hide but one of us stands by the side wall next to the door. Then once they open the door we clock them, steal their guns, and we're out."

"You make it sound so easy," said Billy.

"Trust me," said Bob.

The three of them agreed that Burt should be the one to hide next to the wall while the other two crouched behind the beer barrels. An hour went by, and they hadn't come down to check on them. Two hours went by and still nothing. The three got bored and closed their eyes but still remained in the same spots, only Burt now sat with his back against the wall.

Then they heard footsteps coming down the stairs. The three came to attention and prepared themselves mentally for a fight. Burt bent his knees, and held his fists up. The rattling of keys could be heard as the person behind the door tried to find the right one.

The lock turned and the door slowly creaked open, and the body of a man stepped forward. In an instant, Burt jumped the man and tackled him to the ground. Billy and Bob came out and hustled to aid Burt, ready for a fight.

"That'll show you," said Burt.

He looked at the man's face and was shocked. It was not the face of either one of the two culprits; rather it was Kasper who was shaking.

"Kasper, what are you doing here?" asked Burt.

"Those men fell asleep and I have to prepare for tomorrow and I needed to restock the shelves. I didn't know they had locked you three down here," said Kasper.

Burt helped Kasper to his feet and they made their way up the stairs. They saw the two men, who were out cold sleeping on top of one of the pool tables.

"Unbelievable," said Burt again. "I have seen this scene in my dreams before."

Billy and Bob gave Burt a funny look then took their guns back, and tossed Burt his.

"Take them to the jailhouse behind my office building. Let them sleep it off and I'll deal with them in the morning," said Burt.

Billy and Bob threw the men over their shoulders still sleeping, and carried them over to the jailhouse where the two slept for the rest of the night.

5: CONSTABLE BURT

B urt woke up agitated from sleeping in his uncomfortable office
chair. His head hurt from last night's fall, he'd slept little, and to
make matters worse, his dreams had returned. Only the pool table
scene was gone, the rest remained as normal: he saw himself in gunfights,
trains robberies, escaping prison, a man pointing his gun at him and shooting, and finished with overlooking water with a woman by his side. He
grabbed his whiskey flask that rested on his desk, took a long sip, and then
set it down. He stood up abruptly and kicked his chair back before walking
out the door to the jailhouse.

Rather than the jailhouse being comprised of metal bars, it was a
simple wooden shed, big enough for four people to sit and stand. The only
furniture was two wooden chairs. Burt approached the jailhouse door,
shuffled the keys around and found the right one. He slid the key into its
hole, turned it, and opened the door staring at the men.

"I consider myself a just man, a righteous man, but what you two
did last night was not acceptable and punishment is in order. You see, my
father was keeper of the peace for many years. He taught me that every
man is innocent until proven guilty. Well men, you two are both guilty,"
said Burt.

Billy King and Andy quickly kneeled. "We're sorry sir, we had a few too many to drink last night and this was our first run in with the law, we ask forgiveness," pleaded Andy.

"You can trust us, were sober now Constable," said Billy King.

Burt took a deep breath and opened the door to let them out. "I best not see you two around here any longer, as long as I am in charge there will be peace," Burt said and both men exited the jailhouse.

As Burt closed the door, his back turned from the men. Without hesitation Andy clocked Burt on top of his bruised head while Billy bent down and grabbed both of Burt's ankles. Burt was unfazed this time and did not fall, instead he threw a right elbow into Andy's nose and broke loose from Billy King's grip, and then kicked out at the man's forehead. Burt's heart was beating fast but he was focused. He looked into the scared eyes of both men, pulled out his gun and decided he'd enough of them; he shot both in the chest, instantly killing them.

Burt froze, *What did I do?* he thought. *Self-defense, self-defense, that's what it was*, he told himself.

It was not long after that Billy Stiles and Bob Brown were on the scene to check on Burt. They both looked at the two dead men and the smoke still trickling out of Burt's gun.

"You murdered them in cold blood?" Bob asked.

"He wouldn't do that," Billy responded for Burt.

"They attacked me, so I had to defend myself," Burt explained.

Bob searched the pockets of the two men for identification. Andy had a note in his pants pocket while Billy King had only a few coins. Bob unfolded the note and read it out loud:

"*$50 reward for stealing ten cattle for me.*

Signed,

Three Fingered Jack"

Burt and Billy laughed.

"Who calls themselves Three Fingered Jack?" asked Billy.

Bob looked away as if hoping not to have to answer, then refolded the paper and handed it to Burt. Burt noticed Bob's awkwardness, and as he placed the note in his pants pocket, he asked, "$50? You're telling me an outlaw gets paid more for one job than I do in half a year. We might have to pay a visit one day to this Three Fingered Jack fellow."

Over the next couple of days, Burt was praised by the townspeople for putting an end to the cowboys' lives. They believed when word got out about what had happened that their town would be safer. And over those days there was relative peace. Burt was seen as a tough guy who couldn't be messed with, yet he was still maturing.

Burt continued his work collecting brawl fees, transporting prisoners to awaiting trains headed to either the Tombstone or Yuma prisons, and being at the ready when needed. He put any jailbirds to work sweeping the town's streets and shoveling horse manure. From time to time he looked at that note. For a year he had a hard time grasping that an outlaw could make that much.

* * *

It was now November 1898. Burt was notified of an unsuccessful robbery attempt of some cattle aboard a Southern Pacific train by three men. Burt arranged for Billy and Bob to join him to find the men. First, they headed to the scene of the crime.

"Which way did they head?" Burt asked the train conductor.

"Northwest toward those mountains," the train conductor pointed.

The three men rode fast before sundown hoping to catch the men by surprise. It had recently rained leaving a thin layer of water on the ground.

"Look there," Billy stopped and shouted, "muddy hoofprints leading to between those rocky hills."

"Let's wait fellas, if we really want to surprise them, we should wait until the sun sets, and they have lit their campfire. They won't know what hit them," said Burt.

The three found a safe hidden section on one of the hills underneath a large boulder and stored their horses. Then, they slowly climbed up the rocky incline to scope out the outlaw's exact location. Burt was first to spot them, three men resting on the ground drinking alcohol. Their camp was located next to a small stream. The one thing that stood out to Burt was how well dressed the cowboys were. Everything from their hats, to their vests and boots appeared new.

"Outlawing looks like it paid these men well," said Burt.

Not long after, the sun settled and the cowboys lit a fire for the night. They sang songs, drank, and cleaned their guns as the tranquil sound of water flowed in the stream.

Burt and his men waited for things to quiet down more before surprising them. The last thing they wanted was to allow them to make an easy escape.

"What's the plan Constable?" Bob asked.

"The art of distraction of course," Burt replied. "We'll slowly creep down the rocks and get within twenty-five feet of them. We'll grab some small rocks and throw them off in the distance toward the stream. This will cause them to get up and look in that direction. When they do, we'll sneak up right behind them, guns at the ready. We need to be quiet though, there's a full moon tonight and the visibility will be good for them."

Billy and Bob nodded and the three made their way down the hill slowly avoiding making any sudden noises while zigzagging their way between the large rocks and boulders.

"All right men, it's time," Burt whispered.

The three bent over and picked up some small rocks. "1, 2, 3," Burt and they threw their rocks as far as they could. A couple hit the water making a sudden splash.

The men who were comfortably watching the fire immediately stood up. "What was that," said one of the men. They pulled out their guns and slowly walked toward the noise. Burt, Billy, and Bob quietly approached from behind, not more than 25 feet now.

Burt spoke first, "Hands up boys, and drop your guns."

The cowboys put their hands up and didn't move. The one on the left was tall, the middle one short, and the one on the right skinny. The one in the middle looked back at the Burt, while the other two kept their eyes forward.

"I said guns down!" Burt demanded as the three walked backward slowly toward them.

The cowboys slowly put their guns down on the ground and kept their hands up.

"Now on your knees, you are under arrest," Burt ordered as they closed in.

The three cowboys dropped to their knees as Burt, Billy, and Bob kicked their guns away and tied their hands together behind their backs with rope.

"Well done, Constable," said the man in the middle.

"Have we met before?" Burt asked noticing something odd about the man's right hand. He only had three fingers.

"Ha, only in your dreams," the man said sarcastically. "No, we have not met, but your reputation is well known."

The cowboys were escorted to the awaiting horses under the boulder. More ropes were tied around their necks which linked each man individually to one of the horse's saddles. Burt, Billy, and Bob made quick work releasing the outlaw's horses to go free before hoping onto their own horses, and made the long journey back to the Willcox jailhouse.

The full moon lit their way back to Willcox indicated by the string of lights on the horizon. The man with the three fingers was tied to Burt's saddle. He was a short, but well-built man with a dark, black mustache and wide-brimmed hat.

"How much money would you men of gotten if you'd been successful in stealing those cattle?" Burt asked the man.

"$2 per cow, so around $20 each even split," the man replied. The man didn't miss seeing Burt's eyes lit up a bit.

"What's happened to your hand cowboy?" Burt asked.

"My name is Jack Dunlop, but my friends call me, Three Fingered Jack," he answered. "I lost two of my fingers in a gunfight; shot right off clean by a drunken Mexican."

"Well consider yourselves lucky we didn't kill you, Jack," Burt spit on the ground.

"Why you so interested in how much we could have made? You want in or something?" Jack asked.

Burt pulled out his whiskey flask, and took a swig. "No," Burt paused again to take another sip. "If I'd worked that job, I wouldn't have failed like you. I've met enough outlaws in my day to know not what to do."

Jack frowned at Burt and asked, "Oh yeah? What would you have done differently?"

"For starters, you don't attempt a robbery unless it's been planned out: attacking at the opportune moment, giving jobs to each of your men, knowing where to make a quick exit, and most importantly you sure don't ride off in the direction where it recently rained since your hoofprints were easily spotted," Burt pointed at the ground revealing those same prints still visible from the full moon.

Instead of answering, Jack called out to Bob, "What do you think over there, Bob is he right?

"Quiet, Jack. Burt, don't listen to this liar," Bob called.

"You two know each other?" asked Burt.

"I may have run a couple robberies with him in the past, but the past is the past, and now I am the law," said Bob.

"I wouldn't have lost my fingers if it wasn't for you," Jack growled.

"Quiet. I'm not listening to you two argue all the way to jail," Burt admonished.

"Broke out of my share of jails in my time, hope it's secure," said Jack.

"Your time, Burt questioned, "how old are you?"

Jack slowed his footsteps a little bit causing the rope around his neck to stretch and forcing Burt to slow down his horse.

"Twenty-six, and making loads of money. You men should really consider joining us, even you, Bob. Together, we could run the West," Jack said passionately.

Burt scoffed at his remarks, and tugged on the rope around Jack's neck before saying, "The last thing we'd do is join you," with a stern look in his eye.

Burt, Billy, and Bob took the three fugitives to the Willcox jailhouse where Constable Burt would house them until he decided what to do with them.

6: OUTLAW BURT

By mid-morning Burt was woken by a loud banging sound on the front door of his office. He'd slept a little better last night but the dreams continued. He'd spent another night away from home which happened on occasion when the jailhouse was occupied. He suspected the banging was his wife wanting to know if he was okay. Burt got up and opened the door.

Only it wasn't his wife, rather it was Billy out of breath, "They escaped – somehow they escaped." Billy caught his breath and continued, "They left this note for you."

Burt couldn't believe it. He took the note from Billy and read:

I told you to make sure it was secure. Now, kindly stay out of our way, or join us and make loads of money. Bob will know how to find us.

Before Burt could respond to the note or to Billy, his wife Lola entered the office out of breath as well. "Burt, where have you been?" Lola asked.

"Not now Lola, three fugitives are out there, they just escaped the jailhouse," said Burt.

Lola hugged her husband and said, "I was just worried about you that's all. I haven't seen you in days. Don't leave me now."

"I have to Lola, if I don't find these men, they will cause chaos in our town and others," Burt said.

Just then Bob walked in, "You won't be able to find them, at least not right now. They have various hideouts in the desert, and only pop into towns when they're bored to spend their money at brothels and saloons. Once they run low on money they will rob again. We need to be patient, they will turn up again, and we can take care of them then."

Burt shook his head, "How do we know we can trust you, Bob? You were once one of them."

"Because I'm the one who knows them the best, and I'm your best chance of capturing them," Bob responded.

Burt scoffed, and then paused before turning around and grabbing his flask off his desk. He took a long sip of whiskey. "Fine then, patience it is," Burt said as he set the flask down. "What were the names of the other two men so I know who else we need to capture besides Jack?" asked Burt.

"The tall one was Bravo Juan Yoas, and the skinny one was George Owens who has a brother that normally tags along but didn't this time. His name is Louis," Bob responded.

* * *

A few months later, in January 1899, Burt received a promotion. Sheriff Scott White appointed Burt to Deputy Sheriff of Cochise County. He still held his position of Constable of Willcox. He was now responsible for enforcing law and order to a much larger area consisting of various ranches and settlements, including more saloons, brothels, and gambling houses. Sheriff Scott White felt the county needed someone with a tough guy reputation, and Burt filled that void.

With more territory came more issues. Burglaries, murders, attempted murders occurred almost on a daily basis, and Burt was only one man. He needed help. He enlisted both Billy and Bob to be his deputies and help keep the peace in the region. The community supported Burt, but one day in December 1899, things began to change for Burt. He was becoming worn out from the overwhelming responsibility. To make matters worse, he kept drinking and drinking, trying to knock himself out long enough so as not to deal with those consistent dreams. The more he drank though, the more vivid his dreams became, and it was severely affecting his work.

The dream with the gunfights became more real, as he became rich after trains robberies and then there was the thrill of escaping prison, and finally that man pointing a gun at Burt and shooting as he dodged the bullet when someone else started shooting back. Lastly, before overlooking the water with a woman by his side, he spoke to a man who called himself Roosevelt. The vividness of his dreams only made him lose more sleep.

He became cranky and irritable, and his marriage was on the brink of collapse. Sheriff Scott White started growing weary of Burt; he suspected Burt was becoming more of a friend to the outlaws than enemy. As a result, he gave Burt a warning, which did not sit well with Burt.

After a long argument between Burt and Scott, Burt headed for Kasper Hauser's saloon. He spent a few hours drinking heavily before going home. Upon arriving home, he and his wife had words and Burt eventually telling her, "Were done." He then walked out and went to his Willcox office to sleep. What happened next on that December day would change the course of Burt's reputation in the West for the rest of history.

Burt walked to the front door of his office and found a note had been nailed to the door. He ripped the paper off and examined it. Only his eyes had a hard time focusing because he was drunk. He needed to sit down so he could focus. Burt read the note:

At one time in the past I gave you the opportunity to join us, well now is your last chance. Meet us at the O.K. Corral in Tombstone in two days at high noon.

Just then, Sheriff Scott White slammed the door open and said, "You're drunk again? I've had it with you, you're fired."

Burt was too drunk to understand what had just happened. All he heard was the Sheriff yelling, and from the look on his face Burt decided to pick up his flask and throw it at him. Scott easily dodged it, then pulled out his gun and aimed it at Burt.

"This is it isn't it?" asked Burt.

"This is what?" Scott replied.

"The moment of my awakening," said Burt as he stood up and rested his hand on his cherished gun sitting in its holster.

"Think about what you are doing, Burt," said Scott.

"Oh, I have thought long enough," Burt began to pull his gun from its holster.

In an immediate attempt of self-defense, Scott fired a warning shot over Burt's head.

However, Burt felt this was attempted murder. *Bang* – Burt shot at Scott hitting him directly in the head and killing him instantly. Instead of reacting to what he'd just done, Burt blacked out and fell asleep at his desk.

Upon hearing the gunshots, Billy and Bob rode their horses as quickly as they could toward the sound. They quickly realized the shots came from the direction Burt's office, and the jailhouse.

Billy was first to get off his horse and enter the office. "What the heck happened?" Billy yelled in horror.

Burt did not respond; he was snoring.

Bob walked in next, and put his hand over his mouth in shock at the scene in front of him. Billy stepped over Scott's dead body and slowly approached Burt who continued sleeping in his chair, his gun resting on top of the desk. Billy walked slowly not wanting to make any sudden noises for fear of startling his longtime friend causing Burt to fire at him next. He quietly grabbed the gun off the desk, and then tapped Burt on the shoulder.

Burt still would not wake up. Bob looked to his right and saw a full water pail on the ground. He picked it up and dumped it over Burt's head, immediately waking him up.

"Huh? What? I was sleeping, why would you do that?" asked Burt.

"More like why would you do that?" Bob pointed to the dead body.

"No, what? I would never." Burt paused for a while before continuing, "You know what? He deserved it."

"Burt, you're not thinking straight," Billy argued.

"Hush, Billy," Burt grabbed the note that had been nailed to the door off of his water-soaked desk. "In my hand here is our ticket to live a better life. We'll make more money than we ever thought imaginable. And we won't have to deal with any rough and tough sheriffs anymore because I will be the last one the West will ever see. You both need to join me and go to Tombstone, for we have a ticket to our freedom," Burt told them.

"What note, where?" Billy responded.

Bob turned to Billy and said, "He's talking about Three Fingered Jack and his gang. I'm guessing that he wants us to meet him in Tombstone. The way I see this situation is that we will be considered accomplices in this murder. So we'd better leave town soon or we'll have a mob on our hands."

Billy was still holding Burt's gun but pointed it down. He contemplated arresting Burt in that moment but he feared Bob would not take his side. "We can't just leave, we have a life here," said Billy.

Burt rose swiftly and knocked the gun out of Billy's hand and pointed it at him.

"Billy, you're my best friend. I need you trust me and stay by my side like you always have," said Burt.

At first, Billy said nothing, and just stared at Burt. He weighed his options. He decided that he didn't want to be killed, so he agreed to Burt's terms. "I'm with you Burt," he said with no emotion.

Burt smiled and Bob let out a big sigh and shook his head, "I guess it's back to outlawing."

While the coast was still clear, they buried Scott outside the jailhouse and cleaned up the scene before heading to Tombstone. Scott was only buried under a thin layer of dirt but Burt felt with the sun being so warm it would harden quickly. *There's no way they'll find him*, Burt thought.

7: JACK OF ALL TRADES

Burt, Billy, and Bob arrived at the O.K. Corral in Tombstone where Burt and Billy had once worked as kids. It was hot, and the sun was beating down on them. It was noon, but no Three Fingered Jack or member of his gang were around. They waited and waited, and nothing happened.

Billy started getting impatient, "You brought us all the way out here for nothing?"

"He'll be here," Bob reassured them.

Just then, footsteps approached from behind them, and then a voice, "Sorry boys, I had to spend last night in jail for an old horse theft charge. Instead of escaping I decided to get a good night's rest."

The three turned around and immediately recognized Three Fingered Jack who reached up and adjusted his hat with his three fingers. "It's way too hot out here to be standing around. We got business to do. Follow me to Big Nose Kate's Saloon," Jack said.

As they made their way to the saloon, Jack talked with Burt, "I didn't think you'd come.""It's time for a change, we're all ready to make more money," said Burt.

"What caused the change?" asked Jack.

Burt hesitated to answer but then came out with it, "I killed Sheriff Scott White two days ago. There's no turning back now, might as well get rich while on the run."

Jack nodded and responded, "Bout time someone took care of that old man. Burt, you are clearly a man of power and someone that people look up to as a leader. That's why I'm appointing you leader of my gang. With you in charge we will run the West."

Burt's chest puffed out as he filled with confidence. His new appointed leadership role made him grin ear to ear. He looked back at Billy and said, "Happy to be in charge, but I'm making Billy Stiles my number two."

Billy overheard and gulped as they stopped in front of Big Nose Kate's Saloon.

"You're in charge, and if you want Billy as your number two then he is. Would you like to meet the rest of your gang?" asked Jack.

They walked into the saloon which was full of men surrounding the bar and pool tables. As they entered, everyone stopped and looked and began whispering to one another. Clearly, Burt's reputation stretched all the way to Tombstone; and to their knowledge he was still Deputy Sheriff of Cochise County, and Constable of Willcox. Big Nose Kate was working the bar and also noticed her new customers.

I've seen this woman before, Burt thought.

Jack led them to one of the pool tables where three men were focused on a game. While Bob already knew who they were, Jack pointed out the men to Burt and Billy.

"This here is Bravo Juan Yoas, and Louis and that's George Owens," Jack indicated.

Burt and Billy shook their hands before being interrupted by a woman's voice from behind them asking, "Drinks boys?"

Burt got a better look at Kate. She was a little older than him, tall with dark hair and looked very familiar, only he couldn't figure it out. "Have we met?" Burt asked.

She smiled and responded, "Only in your dreams sweetheart. The name is Kate, owner of this saloon."

"But you don't have a big nose, why do they call you Big Nose Kate?" asked Burt.

Kate looked at Jack and said, "Wow, this one is a charmer." She then looked back at Burt, "I guess I'm always trying to get my nose into everyone's business, don't understand why." She then paused, "So what brings you three sorry-looking fellows here with Eight Fingered Jack and his boys? Killed anyone recently?"

"Three fingers," Jack announced.

"Well, you see ..." Burt started but was stopped by Billy's hand on his shoulder.

"She does have a big nose," said Billy.

Kate smiled, and walked away.

Burt kept starring at her as she made her way behind the bar. He put his hand on Billy's shoulder and asked him, "Did we see her once at the Wyatt Earp gunfight when we were kids?"

"Oh, who knows Burt. Stay focused, you're married man," said Billy.

The men stayed at the saloon for hours drinking, laughing, playing pool, and getting to know one another. Burt was seated next to Jack as they watched Bob and Billy duel out an intense back and forth pool game.

"The easy money seems to be in cattle rustling. I grew up in this town and know of a place off to the south that will be easy picking," Burt suggested.

"Were with you boss. But there's just one problem in our way, Jeff Milton is in town," said Jack.

"Who's Jeff Milton?" asked Burt.

"He's a former Texas Ranger, and now Deputy U.S. Marshal. He has a reputation for never backing down. He resides in Nogales," Jack responded.

"Well, I ain't scared of nobody. Even the smartest of men can be distracted. Leave him to me. Tomorrow we'll do the job, and easy it will be," Burt said confidently.

"Well, aren't you a Jack of All Trades, which is funny because my name is Jack," Jack laughed.

Burt did not understand his reference, but instead was distracted by Kate again standing in front of them.

"Tell me about that Kate woman right quick before I turn in for the night," whispered Burt.

Jack responded, "She was once married to Doc Holliday, you know, the dentist gunslinger guy close to Wyatt Earp."

Burt nodded and looked over at Jack, "Yep, I know the guy, he died years back, but not before killing my friend, Frank McLaury in a famous gunfight many years ago. So, that's how I know her. I saw her that day, and here we are."

Just as he finished, Kate appeared and sat down on Burt's lap. Burt froze, not knowing exactly what to do. "Last call for drinks boys," Kate announced. She then whispered into Burt's ear, "These boys will get you into trouble, watch your back." Kate then kissed Burt on the cheek before getting up.

He was still frozen, and his thoughts conflicted with one another. He did not know if he should shoot her then and there for being with the man involved in the killing of his friend, or ask her when he could see her again. Instead, he did nothing. He was tired and wanted to turn in. He got up and announced to his men, "Tomorrow, we discuss our first hit. Billy and Bob, I suggest you come with me and we find a room at a hotel tonight."

As the three reached the door, Burt was stopped by a young teenage boy who saw Burt's Silver Star on his vest.

"Sir, cattle keep disappearing off my family's farm. We own the biggest farm in the county. Can you help us?"

"Where's the farm located kid?" Burt asked.

"South of here in Nogales, about a day's ride, you can't miss the big sign when you get there, *Nelson Farm*," said the boy.

"I'll see what I can do kid, thanks for the information," Burt responded.

The three men exited, with Burt smiling. His mind was now consumed with plotting his first cattle rustling at the Nelson Farm.

While Billy and Bob slept well, Burt did not. The same visions continued. He tossed and turned all night, and at one point yelled out, "No!"

Billy quickly covered his mouth. "Shh, let's not get caught out here because of your night terrors," whispered Billy.

With first daylight, the heat of the sun roared in. Burt was thirsty, hungry, and had a headache. "One of you fetch us some water and bread," Burt instructed.

Bob got up and walked away.

"After all these years, who would have thought we would be back here," Billy said.

"It seems like yesterday that *Honest John* Montgomery was yelling at me for not showing up on time," said Burt.

"So, what's the plan boss?" Billy asked.

"We're heading to Nogales today to steal cattle from the Nelson Farm. Once we sell them at auction, we will collect our first cash," said Burt.

"But what about Jeff Milton, what are we going to do about him?" asked Billy.

"Oh, leave him to me. I am very much so looking forward to meeting Mr. Milton," Burt smiled.

8: THE NELSON RANCH

The men reached the outskirts of Nogales late in the afternoon; a bustling town filled with mostly Mexicans and white settlers. Burt and Billy went into town first searching for Jeff Milton. Burt found a resident and asked for his whereabouts. Seeing Burt's Silver Star badge, the man felt obligated to answer. He directed them toward the far end of town to the sheriff's building. Burt also took the opportunity to ask where the Nelson Ranch was located. He obliged and pointed West.

Burt and Billy tied up their horses in front of the sheriff's building and walked in. Inside were two desks, one on the left, and one on the right, both occupied by men. A jail which was visible through the back window was housed in the back of the building.

"I am Deputy Sheriff Burt Alvord of Cochise County and Constable of Willcox. I'm looking for Deputy U.S. Marshal Jeff Milton," Burt said with authority.

The man on the right answered, "I'm Jeff Milton."

Burt stared at him for a moment. He had a thick, black mustache and wore a white long-sleeved button-down shirt, his shotgun rested on top of his desk.

Burt nodded, "This is my Deputy, Billy Stiles."

Billy shook his hand.

"What brings you two to Nogales?" asked Jeff.

"We've been directed by Sheriff Scott White to investigate some cattle rustling out this way. We have learned of a plot that one might go down today and we wanted you to stop it by staking out the farm," said Burt.

"Not sure why the Sheriff didn't just telegraph me. What farm is it?" asked Jeff.

"We're having a hard time remembering. What farms around here house the most cattle?" asked Billy.

"Well, there is the Nelson Farm, Smith Farm, Davidson Farm, any of those sound familiar?" asked Jeff.

"Smith Farm, that's definitely it. We need you to head out there now on the orders of the Sheriff," Burt said.

Jeff Milton was not the kind of person to question a direct order. He quickly got up, grabbed his shotgun, and exited the building along with his deputy. Burt and Billy followed.

Just as they jumped up onto their horses, Jeff asked, "Aren't you boys coming too?"

"We have orders to stay put. If you apprehend the outlaws, we'll meet you back here to personally take them back to Willcox," Burt replied.

Jeff tipped his hat at the two and rode off toward Smith Farm to the east. Burt and Billy hopped onto their horses smiling, and relieved that the Smith Farm was in the opposite direction of the Nelson Farm.

"I told you I'd take care of him," Burt grinned at Billy.

An hour or so later, Burt and Billy met up with the five other gang members: Three Fingered Jack, Bravo Juan Yoas, Bob Brown, George Owens as well as his brother Louis. They remained on the outskirts of town riding slowly so as not to attract attention; for the amount of the dirt the horses would kick into the air would surely draw some eyes. Not much later, they came across a big sign that read: *Nelson Farm*. Hundreds of cows and bulls could be seen roaming the grass fields with no people in sight.

"Alright men," Burt announced. "It's almost dusk, the best time for this. Billy, Jack, Bravo, Bob, and me will nab two cattle each. George and Louis you keep a look out for anything suspicious. George – stay here by this sign. Louis – go up ahead about two hundred yards, and take out your matches. If you see anything that might jeopardize us light one match. George, if you see the match whistle loudly twice and we'll stop everything. Oh, and men, go for the young calves, they'll fetch more at auction. Got it?"

"Only two?" Bravo questioned.

"More cattle means more time, it's all about speed, not quantity," Burt replied. Then with a stern look, he added, "And Bravo – don't ever question me again."

All the men nodded and Louis rode off. The men pulled out their ropes and rode in the directions of the nearest ones in sight. Within seconds, they'd all lassoed their first calf, and after a few minutes all five had two calves each. They each tied the lassos to their saddles and all five men met back at the sign. The sun had not yet started to set and Burt knew it would be tough to see soon.

"Yeehaw," Jack yelled, "easy work."

Just then, Burt spotted a light in Louis's direction.

"Trouble men," Burt pointed to the light. Burt looked north in the direction of some small rocky hills. "George, take my calf. Billy, lead the men north quickly but quietly to those hills and hide out. I'll get Louis and meet you there."

The others left immediately as Burt rode fast to Louis. Upon his arrival, Burt asked, "What did you see?"

"See what?" asked Louis.

"What? You lit your match," Burt stated.

"Oh no, I just needed a smoke," said Louis.

Without hesitation, Burt knocked Louis's cigarette out of his hand and onto the ground and asked him, "Do you realize that you almost jeopardized this whole thing? Did you not hear a word I said earlier?"

Louis hesitated, and then said, "Sorry boss, couldn't help myself." He then pulled out a tall whiskey bottle from his bag and asked, "Can I offer you a drink for my shortcoming?"

Burt grabbed the bottle out of his hands. "Smoking might be our downfall one day, and no, I will not take just a drink, I'll take the whole thing. Consider that your punishment," said Burt.

It was now almost pitch dark, but Burt led Louis in the direction of his men. The two of found the men from the sounds of the calves.

"What happened boss?" Jack asked.

"It seems that Louis here needed a smoke. No trouble to us," said Burt. "Men, take the calves back to Tombstone while Billy and I pay Jeff Milton another visit. Good job tonight."

The other men headed to Tombstone while Burt and Billy went to town to find the nearest hotel for the night before we see Milton. While in their room, Burt finished off the whiskey bottle, and then blacked out on his bed. A few hours later, Burt woke up in a deep sweat and was breathing heavily. The dreams continued.

Billy got up to get him a wet towel, but when he returned Burt had gone back to sleep.

The next morning, instead of heading to the sheriff's building, Burt wanted to scope out the train station for a potential future train hit. He talked to one of the ticket sellers and asked for the upcoming train schedules. The conductor handed Burt a copy of the schedules for the next few months. Burt folded the paper and placed it in his pants pocket before he and Billy went to find Jeff Milton. They parked their horses, walked inside and there he was, at his desk, but sleeping probably from a long night. His deputy was not present.

"Wake up, Mr. Milton," Billy called.

Jeff did not move. Burt then slammed his fist down on the desk waking Jeff up instantly.

"Sorry to bother you Marshal, but did you find the outlaws last night?" Burt asked.

Jeff rubbed the crust from his eyelids and responded, "No, no outlaws out there last night. Seems that Sheriff Scott White was wrong. I sent him a telegraph last night but haven't heard back."

The front door opened, and his deputy entered looking just as tired as Jeff.

"Word came back about your message to Sheriff Scott White. It says he's been missing for a few days and that now Deputy Sheriff Burt Alvord is in charge," said the deputy.

Burt grinned from ear to ear. *This is too easy*, he thought to himself.

"Well, that's you," said Jeff. "Best be headed back to Willcox and see if you can find him."

"Will do, but listen up, you and I need to work as a team. We might telegraph you in the future if we need assistance. We just ask that you respond back in a timely manner," said Burt.

"Of course, good luck to you both. I hope you find the sheriff," said Jeff.

Burt and Billy tipped their hats and walked out. They then headed toward Tombstone for a quick trip before returning to Willcox.

9: EASY MONEY

Burt and Billy met up with their gang the next morning. They were still in possession of the stolen calves. Jack had learned of an upcoming auction that afternoon and explained to Burt that it was better for only two of them to be at the auction, and they could meet up afterward in Big Nose Kate's Saloon where everyone would get their cut of the money. Burt agreed, and directed Jack and his trusted friend Billy to go to the auction while he and the rest of the men, went to the saloon.

While they waited at the saloon, Louis, George, Bravo, and Bob found an open pool table while Burt locked eyes with Kate. She was working the bar fixing drinks for a few men. One man in particular appeared to be giving her trouble.

"Kate … *hiccup* … I'm not asking you again, hurry up with my drink … *hiccup*," the man ordered.

The man was wobbling somewhat in his chair and had the hiccups. Burt went over, tapped the man on the shoulder and asked Kate, "Is this man giving you trouble?"

Kate did not answer, but had a worried look in her eyes. The man stared up at Burt's big round face; he was too drunk to feel intimidated.

"*Hiccup* … what's your problem buddy?" the man drawled. He then turned to Kate, pounded his fist on the bar, "Hurry up with my drink."

Burt grabbed the man by the neck collar and pulled him off his bar stool. The stool slammed on the ground, causing everyone to look in their direction. Burt's gang's hands hovered just above their guns sitting in their holsters ready to protect Burt. The man's feet thudded on the ground as Burt dragged him to the exit.

"Stop!" the guy yelled.

Burt said nothing in return and refused to loosen his grip as the drunk struggled to reach behind him. Burt stopped at the door, let go of him for a moment, but only to reach back with his left hand and punch the man squarely across his right cheek. The guy's tooth flew out of his mouth and rolled across the floor. Burt then held him again by his collar and used his other hand to hold him by a belt loop. He lifted him into the air as everyone in the saloon froze, shocked by Burt's strength. He then proceeded to throw the man outside with a loud crash. Then, like nothing had happened, Burt walked up to the knocked over bar stool, righted it up off the ground and sat down. Kate held the beer the man had ordered and set it down in front of Burt.

Kate looked a little shocked herself but blushed at the same time. "This one's on the house," she said with a smile.

"Glad he's on our side," Bravo said to the gang.

Burt sat quietly for about ten minutes sipping his beer trying to find the courage to speak to Kate. He held onto his glass, looked at the liquid, and proceeded to finish the beer in one final chug. As he set the glass down, he finally spoke. "Kate, something has been on my mind," Burt started, looking down at his empty glass.

"What? Another beer?" Kate questioned.

"Tell me about you and Doc Holliday," said Burt.

"Why do you need to know?" Kate asked.

"Because the problem is, I like you, but he killed my friend when I was young in the Wyatt Earp shootout here years back," Burt explained.

Kate hesitated, surprised by the question. "Um … well, Doc was my first love, my best friend. But after the shootout he changed, and left for a life of fame and glory following Wyatt Earp around the country. Though I still loved him, I couldn't be with him. I saw him the day before he died in Colorado. But, that's all in the past now, it's hard to believe it has been twelve years," a small tear ran down her right cheek.

Burt reached over and wiped it away, "I didn't mean to make you sad."

Burt decided to change subjects and sat at the bar for the next hour talking to Kate as his gang ate and played pool. Jack and Billy walked through the door, each sporting a big grin. Burt met them at the pool table with the rest of the gang.

"Easy money. Got top dollar for all of them, $40 total. How do you want to split it up boss?" Bravo asked Burt.

"$5 for each of us, which leaves $5 to invest in new supplies," Burt instructed.

The men smiled at their boss, and were somewhat surprised that he didn't take more of a cut for himself. Burt knew how to influence people. By doing this he not only established his role on the gang as the boss, but he knew the men were less likely to stab him in the back.

Once the money was in Burt's hands, his head grew bigger filling with thoughts about how to get even more. He felt that a train robbery would yield a better return. But then realized that he had to return to Willcox with Billy and Bob to find a solution to the blood he had on his hands. His mind raced with ideas, and he formed a plan.

The men were about to leave, but Burt called them back. "Now you boys have fun, and don't spend all of it too quick. We'll meet back here in two weeks to go over plans for a train robbery. Billy and Bob, we'll head to Willcox tomorrow. I think I may have a solution to our problem."

Days later, Burt, Billy, and Bob were back in the Willcox sheriff's office. Word had spread quickly of their return which led droves of people to congregate outside, not to hang them, but rather to ask for their help.

"What's the plan boss?" Billy asked.

Burt stepped outside to speak to the townspeople. A voice from the crowd yelled, "Where's the Sheriff?" Burt put his hands in the air to silence the crowd. He announced, "My citizens of Willcox. I know you all need help, but I'm afraid I have some bad news. Sheriff Scott White is dead. We caught the man who shot him yesterday, and put a quick end to him in a shootout on the outskirts of town."

The crowd began talking among themselves, and Burt put his hands up again.

The voice of another man spoke out, "So what does that mean then? Are you now the Sheriff?"

"People, people – that is not up to me. I have some more news. As of today, I have officially retired from my duties," Burt advised.

The crowd was now restless and upset. "We need you Burt," said a woman.

Just then, Burt's wife approached him and pulled him into the office while the crowd watched. Billy and Bob were still inside.

"Lola, what are you doing here? I told you we're done," said Burt.

Lola hugged him tight and said, "I don't know, once I heard you were back, I had to come see you."

Burt escorted her out back to not make a scene.

"We're through. I've moved on. Besides, I'm in love with someone else now," said Burt.

Lola looked at him intently, and then slapped him across the face. Tears ran down her face as she yelled, "After everything I did for you – good luck finding someone that will deal with your night terrors, or even worse, your drinking." She then reached back to hit him again but before she could Billy grabbed her wrist. Billy then let go, but not before she spit in Burt's face before storming out.

"Well, that went well," Bob said as Burt wiped the spit off his face.

"The crowd outside is growing larger boss, what are you going to do?" asked Billy.

Burt walked outside again, and put his hands up. "People hush now. Your new Sheriff should be arriving in town any day now. You'll just have to trust me. In the meantime, I will help some of you until he gets here," Burt announced.

Inside, Billy and Bob overheard every word. "What the heck is he doing?" Bob asked Billy.

"If you knew Burt like I do, you'd know there's always a solution to every problem. He knew this would happen. Let's just hope no one discovers the truth," said Billy.

Then, outside near the jailhouse a young boy was playing in some loose dirt. The boy's mother looked over to see what he was playing with, and suddenly, she let out a loud scream. "It's a dead body!"

People ran to see who it was. A man uncovered the face and announced, "Its Sheriff Scott White!"

Burt immediately went back inside and locked the door. "This was not part of the plan," Burt thought to himself. People started slamming their fists on the door yelling.

"Draw your weapons," said Bob.

A few gunshots entered the room forcing the three to duck.

"No," said Burt, "I have an escape plan." He leaned down and pulled the rug out from underneath his desk uncovering a trapdoor. He opened it and said, "Get in."

Billy and Bob hesitated for a moment but climbed down first. Burt was last but not before he pulled the rug back over the top of the door as he closed it.

The trapdoor led to a dark, narrow tunnel of dirt, only accessible by crawling.

Bob coughed from the lack of air and asked, "Where does this lead?"

"Just keep going," said Burt.

After a few minutes, Bob was the first to see light. In front of him was a square-shaped board.

From behind, Burt said, "If you see the light push up on the board and exit."

Bob climbed through the opening, followed by Billy, then Burt; all three still on their hands and knees.

"Well, I'll be. We're in the jailhouse," said Bob.

"Yes, now stay low and don't make a peep. I'm the only one with the keys so they can't get in. Scott White told me about this tunnel a while back. It was dug out by some outlaws who killed the sheriff before him. That's how he got the job. The crowd should dissipate by nightfall and once they do, we'll need to steal three horses and leave for Tombstone."

"They'll kill us if they see us," said Bob worried.

"We must have patience then if you don't want to get killed," said Burt.

Billy smiled, knowing Burt had a plan all along. They hid inside the jailhouse up against the door aware that no one could see them as they peeked out through the cracks in the wood. Burt gave them the confidence they needed, and they caught a nap as they waited for nightfall.

10: TUNNELS

The sun had gone down, the moon was out, and crickets were chirping. Not one person could he heard outside. The three men sat on the floor with their backs still against the wall almost shoulder to shoulder exhausted, hungry, and bored. Bob ran his heels back and forth on the ground sliding a light layer of dirt. Billy tossed a pebble up in the air from one hand to the next while Burt's feet rested on top of one of the wooden chairs. He sat thinking about the events that occurred earlier. *There's no turning back now*, Burt thought to himself.

"When are we going to leave?" asked Billy.

"Just because you don't hear nobody outside doesn't mean nobody is there. Billy, take a long look through the cracks to the outside," said Burt.

Billy dropped the pebble, stood up, and looked from side to side a couple times before announcing, "Looks clear."

Burt lifted his feet off the chair, but as they hit the ground, something metallic fell from underneath the chair. Burt grabbed it, and pulled it close to examine it. It was as thin as a nail but much longer with the end being more like a hook. *3FJ* was scratched on the flat side of the nail.

"What you got there?" asked Billy.

"Seems to be how Three Fingered Jack escaped that time with Bravo and George. How nice of him to leave it for us after he got out," Burt smiled.

Burt fit the long nail on the inside of his vest on a strap and took out his keys. He found the correct key and proceeded to try to unlock the door from the inside. However, the lock would not twist no matter how hard he tried. He then looked out the window to make sure no one was watching and proceeded to reach out the window to find the keyhole. The angle was awkward and he dropped the keys, which hit the dirt ground.

"Seriously," Burt uttered.

"Seems like you have one last try with that nail boss," said Billy.

Burt, now annoyed, opened his vest and pulled out the nail.

"Here, let me show you how it's done," Bob said taking the nail out of Burt's hand. "You see, you need to place the end of it at an angle and then, slowly twist until you hear a click."

The door immediately unlocked and Burt was baffled.

"Easy as that?" asked Burt as he took back the nail and placed it under the same chair to keep it hidden.

"Easy to get out of jail, harder to not get caught," replied Bob.

"Speaking of not getting caught, this is the plan. We have to get over to the local corral and steal three horses. It's very similar to the one Billy and I worked at in Tombstone. There's always one man on watch at night for security, but I know how we can sneak in undetected. Follow me," said Burt.

Burt led them behind buildings quickly and thoroughly without being detected. A few people were walking around, but did not seem to notice them. However, in the distance there was a mob of people yelling and holding sticks with fire. Burt, Billy, and Bob stayed low as the mob passed, but not before hearing someone say, "We're burning down the sheriff's office." The three looked at one another with their eyes wide but not before Burt pushed forward knowing that they needed to get out of town quickly.

It wasn't long until they reached their destination, but it wasn't the front entrance. Burt led them to the side of the building and pointed at the ground. It was a three-foot by three-foot circular cast iron plate.

"What is it?" asked Bob.

"A drain where we poured out the old water, it leads to … Burt you're a genius," said Billy.

"Leads to what?" asked Bob.

"Leads inside the corral to the front of the horse stables," said Burt. "Hurry, get in quick."

The drain was not much bigger than the dirt tunnel earlier. Billy led the way, followed by Bob, and then Burt. Billy realized something wasn't right from the start. He could hear faint squeaking sounds. He stopped crawling to get a match out of his pocket. Though the angle was awkward he managed to light it.

"Oh no! It's occupied by rats," Billy said in disgust.

"They don't like fire, keep the match lit and they'll run out," said Burt.

"But they'll run in the direction we need to go which will alert the guard," said Billy.

"We have to take a chance, proceed," said Burt.

Billy continued crawling on one arm with his other hand holding up the lit match. Seconds later, the match went out. Billy scrambled to get another one lit but dropped the matchbox. He felt around for it but couldn't locate it. Instead, his hand touched one a rat's tail and he let out a yell.

"Shh!" said Burt. "Focus for us."

Billy took a deep breath and found the matchbox. He lit another match and proceeded forward. Moments later, they made it to their location. They could hear the rats squeaking as they ran above them.

"Ok, Billy. Now go slow and get your gun at the ready," said Burt.

Billy pulled out his gun, slowly slid the cast iron plate that covered the drain and crawled his way up. His eyes peered around – no one could be detected. Billy grabbed Bob's arm and helped him up, followed by Burt. The three men were now filthy with rat feces and dirt covering their clothes. They looked around and saw no one. Burt crouched down and hurried to the horse stables with Billy and Bob close behind.

"Each of you grab one – hurry," Burt whispered.

They tied saddles onto their horses, and hopped on. They made it no more than ten feet before they were forced to stop. A silhouette of a man, about thirty feet away stood pointing a shotgun at them.

"We'd like to rent these horses. We can pay top dollar," Burt called.

The man slowly walked forward, and Burt tried to see who it was. His appearance was covered by the darkness.

"Get your guns at the ready men," Burt whispered to Billy and Bob. "Put your gun down sir, I am the law around here."

The man only kept walking closer, pointing his shotgun at them and not speaking. He made it within twenty-five feet before a lamp light revealed his features. He had a thick, black mustache.

"Jeff Milton – is that you?" asked Burt.

"Is I. It seems you boys decided to manipulate me, took me for a fool. Now drop your weapons, and get down so I can take you three to the jailhouse," demanded Jeff.

"Let's listen to him boys, don't want to keep disturbing the peace," said Burt.

"We're giving up that easily?" Billy questioned.

"I said guns down!" Jeff yelled.

The three tossed their guns to the ground, and slowly got off their horses. Jeff grabbed the guns, placed one in his holster, and the other two inside his jacket. He then jumped on Billy's horse and held his shotgun in their direction.

"Now, walk in front of me and don't say a word. We're not disturbing these people anymore tonight," said Jeff.

Jeff made them walk down the middle of the main road of town. People quickly noticed, and soon word got out about what was happening. The mob of people about to burn down the sheriff's office stopped as they also heard and hurried to the scene. As the three men marched down the middle of the street, the people clapped and cheered for Jeff Milton. Billy and Bob were appalled by their embarrassment, holding their heads down. Burt held his head up high and smiled. Billy noticed Burt's smile and realized that he was up to something. In a show of gloat, Jeff came up from behind Burt and kicked his back. The people cheered even louder. Burt's grin quickly turned downward. He was now angry, but knew if he reacted a bullet would not only come from Jeff, but any citizen of Willcox The three of them were now back in the jailhouse, just as before. Jeff locked the door using the keys that Burt had left on the ground; he'd forgotten to pick them back up. Before walking away, Jeff said, "In the morning, justice will happen for Sheriff Scott White."

They were sweating, tired, and stunk. Burt watched Jeff through the window and waited for him to go inside the office. But first, Jeff calmed the townspeople, urging them to not shoot the three. Though reluctant, the townspeople listened and left. Jeff then entered the office and shut the door. A light came on through the office window as he lit a lantern.

"Okay boys, I know you think I let you down back there by giving up, but we have another opportunity here," said Burt.

"Were done for, we'll all be dead in the morning," mumbled Bob still embarrassed.

"Get your mind right, Bob. When that lantern burns out, he will mostly likely be asleep inside. We'll wait a little bit, but then I'll crawl back through the tunnel and retrieve our guns and then we'll break out of here with the nail," Burt assured the two.

"Why don't we just get out of here now boss?" asked Billy.

"I need my gun," said Burt.

"The McLaury gun? It's just an old gun, we can get you a new one," Billy argued.

"I'm in charge," Burt folded his arms. He then reached under the same chair and pulled out the nail. "Take this; if something happens to me you two can escape."

Billy took the nail, and nodded before sitting down in one of the chairs. An hour later, the lantern had gone out. Burt waited another hour before figuring it was now or never. He climbed into the dirt tunnel and crawled his way to the office. He made it to the other end with ease but then had to figure out how to open the trapdoor quietly which still had the rug resting on top.

Burt took a deep breath and slowly inched the door open. It barely made a sound but the rug slid hitting the leg of the desk. While the sound was not loud, Burt feared it was loud enough to awaken Jeff. Burt paused and listened. He heard the faint sound of snoring from across the room. He felt confident enough to climb out of the hole but stayed low. It was dark in the office, but not darker than the tunnel. Burt's eyes adjusted quickly and he scanned the room for not only their guns, but for Jeff. His eyes first fell upon Jeff who was sleeping on the floor with his head resting on top of a bag of rice. Burt continued checking out the room hoping he would not have to walk around. He was about to give up when he noticed the three guns sitting on top of his desk, right in front of him. Burt quietly grabbed their weapons, placing his own in its holster, and the other two into his back side underneath his pants. Just as he'd secured the guns, Jeff snored loudly, startling Burt. His heel hit the desk chair making a quiet screech. Burt crouched down really low just as Jeff's eyes opened. But almost immediately his eyes closed again.

Burt quietly slid down the hole, inched the door shut as he threw the rug over at the same time. He let out a deep breath and smiled; then crawled back to the jailhouse to the waiting Billy and Bob poised to make their escape. Again, they used the nail to unlock the door. Burt placed it back under the chair before leaving with Billy and Bob. They took the one and only horse that Jeff had tied up outside the office, and took turns riding and walking together back to Tombstone.

11: FAIRBANK ROBBERY

The journey back to Tombstone took about four days. They survived on a loaf of bread, a canteen of water, and a can of beans they'd stolen from a wagon on their first day of travel. The sun burned their skin and dried out their lips. Burt, however, was on a mission. His eagerness to push forward provided the energy Billy needed to continue on as well. It was the longest four days of their live. They met back up at Big Nose Kate's Saloon two weeks to the day as Burt had instructed.

"What happened?" asked Jack.

"Jeff Milton is what happened. But that won't stop us from our next robbery. We'll always be one step ahead of him," said Burt.

"Were with you Burt," said Jack.

Burt shook his head, pulled out the train schedules from his pocket, and announced to his gang, "Okay men, in three days' time we rob the Southern Pacific train departing from Nogales to Benson. We'll hit it before it makes its scheduled stop in Fairbank."

They all smiled except Billy, who was now questioning why he was doing this. His skin was still beet red and all he could think about was how bad he needed to sleep. He figured though he couldn't leave or they would kill him.

Burt laid out the plan and finished by saying, "Who wants to get rich?" They all cheered in response.

"Kate, fix us some beers please!" Burt called.

Three days later the men were filled with excitement as their horses quickly stamped the ground racing toward the train bolting down the tracks. It was a clear, hot sunny day in the Arizona desert, February 1900. Large trunks of money and silver coins valued in at $20,000 sat in the last caboose car guarded by only two young guards sleeping on their way to the town of Fairbank. Burt Alvord and his gang comprised of Billy Stiles, Bravo Juan Yoas, brothers George and Louis Owens, Three Fingered Jack Dunlop, and Bob Brown closed in to take advantage of the awaiting riches and unsuspecting guards. The gang planned to sneak through the back of the train. Sweat dripped off the brim of Burt's hat did nothing to distract him.

The train showed no sign of stopping. Steam billowed out the smokestack as the engine screamed forward. Three Fingered Jack was first to reach the back of the train. In one swift move, he stood up on top of his horse and jumped victoriously grabbing onto the guardrail. The gang cheered loudly which alerted the two guards who woke up.

"Something ain't right," uttered one of the guards. The other guard opened his flask, took a sip, and closed his eyes ignoring his partner. The alarmed guard stood, rubbed his eyes and looked out the back caboose window. As his eyes began to focus, he was confused momentarily unable to process what he was seeing – a tall white cowboy hat just outside the glass. The hat then turned and revealed the smiling face of Three Fingered Jack who started knocking his revolver on the glass. The guard gasped as he stepped backward tripping over the legs of his sleeping partner. "Get up!" he yelled as he crawled toward his rifle.

Next Bravo Juan Yoas approached the back of the train. Three Fingered Jack reached out with his three fingers and grabbed his arm helping him onto the train. "Bravo!" screamed the gang as he got on. Wasting no time, Bravo pulled out his revolver and kicked the door down in one ferocious stomp of his boot. The two guards held their rifles tightly as they hid behind the trunks expecting a bloody fight.

"Nice kick, you are getting better at this," Jack said in a low voice.

They entered holding their revolvers, loaded and ready to fire. Only nothing happened. It was eerily silent, as if the two guards had left. Instead, the guards continued to lay low. In the middle of the room rested the large trunks of cash and coins. Bravo took a step forward but Jack tugged his arm to stop him. Behind them was a loud thud as Burt stepped onto the train. The two guards peeked out from the sides of the trunks to see the bald, yet intimating strong presence of Burt Alvord. He scratched the top of his bald head before asking, "How many?"

Jack replied, "Two."

Burt stepped forward, his boots stomping loud on the wooden floor which only further intimidated the guards. He announced, "You men ought to think hard about your loved ones right now. Would they want to see you all shot up? The logical move in all this is for both of you to stand up and let us do our job."

The three outlaws stood in a ready stance to fire as the two guards looked at one another with panic-stricken faces. The guard with the flask took a sip before deciding to slowly stand with his hands in the air holding his Winchester. Now with the odds stacked against him, the other guard was obligated to stand as well.

"Yeehaw!" announced the delighted Bravo as he stripped both guards of their firearms. Jack rested his gun on his shoulder as Burt proceeded to open the trunks using the tip of his revolver to verify the treasure. The trunks revealed just what they had come for, loads of cash and silver coins. "A job well done boys!" Burt complimented.

Bravo placed his revolver back in his holster and pointed the two rifles at the guards. "To your knees," he demanded. Without hesitation, both guards dropped to their knees scared, and breathing heavily.

"I smell whiskey!" Jack went over and searched the men's pockets. He pulled out the flask and placed it into his own pocket.

"Stop messing around and help me fill these bags," Burt demanded.

The three quickly stuffed the cash and coins into bags while keeping a keen eye on the guards who were still in shock. The trunks were now empty and the bags were full and heavy. Burt was strong and easily carried his bag. Bravo and Jack were not as fortunate and had to drag their loot across the wooden floor. They had to abandon their rifles on the floor to get the job done. "Hurry up!" yelled Burt from outside the door. Burt then whistled loudly for the rest of the gang to come and help carry the loot and themselves out of there.

But suddenly a door slammed loudly. It came from the other end of the caboose. A man with a thick, black mustache pointing a rifle at Bravo and Jack entered. The two guards quickly exited the scene behind the man and through the door. "The name's Jeff Milton and you men are under arrest," he said.

Burt hearing the words was in shock. Without hesitation, Burt pulled out his revolver, aimed it at Jeff, and effectively hit him in the left shoulder. As Jeff fell, he shot his rifle wildly three times with one bullet shooting clean through Bravo's right buttock.

"I've been hit!" Bravo yelled holding his right butt cheek.

Jack pulled out his revolver as Burt hid behind the wall next to the doorway for cover. Bravo hobbled outside as Jack shot at Jeff three times. Jeff crawled behind the trunks managing to avoid the bullets. Burt moved to the opening and shot his revolver two more times in the direction of the trunks. Jeff's arm was now spilling with blood, and he winced in pain. He managed to unbuckle his belt and fastened a makeshift tourniquet to slow down the bleeding.

Hoping for a quick end to the fight, Jack confidently approached the trunks with his revolver in hand. He moved to the back side of one of the trunks, fired once expecting a direct hit. However, Jeff was gone and there was nothing but a puddle of blood. Burt reloaded as Jack noticed the blood trail. He followed it with his eyes to a couple of whiskey barrels in the corner of the room. Just as Jack's eyes read, *Whiskey* on the barrels Jeff popped up and shot Jack in the chest. Jack fell back and the guard's flask that was in his pocket fell out and clanked to the ground. Burt shot four times hitting the whiskey barrels each time causing them to leak, but still missed hitting Jeff. At that point, Jeff bent back down for safety, but felt light-headed. His eyes closed and he passed out onto the floor causing a loud thud as he splashed into the pool of whiskey. Blood was still spilling from his shoulder.

Burt ran over to Jack, saw that he was still breathing and dragged him to safety outside next to Bravo who was holding his butt in pain. Next to the train, Billy Stiles and Bob Brown waited with the Owens brothers not far behind. Burt dragged Bravo and Jack to the side of the train as Billy and Bob pulled them down and onto their horses. Burt was now angry and decided he needed to make sure Jeff Milton was indeed dead. He walked back into the caboose and observed Jeff lying face down in a pool of blood, but was distracted by the strong smell of whiskey. He could see it still trickling out of the barrels. He looked down and saw the flask from Jack's pocket, and picked it up. Burt opened the cap, bent down, and placed the opening over the stream of whiskey filling it up. Before he stood, he took a long sip. He the realized that the whiskey made it appear that there was more blood than there was. He also noticed that Jeff's chest was not moving indicating to him that he was dead. Burt scoffed, left the caboose carrying all three loot bags to his awaiting horse being pulled by George Owens.

12: SID THE KID

The train stopped at the Fairbank station. All seemed normal until one station worker, sixteen-year-old Sid Mullen, noticed blood dripping to the ground from the caboose. He whistled loudly, signaling to the other men to come over.

"What's wrong?" asked one of the workers.

Sid simply pointed, and the others saw the blood. The men drew their guns, jumped onto the caboose, and walked through the door.

"Hello?" Sid called.

The sound of moaning was coming from near the barrels. Sid walked over, gun at the ready, and to his horror saw Jeff Milton in a pool of blood. Sid holstered his gun and rested a finger by Jeff's nose to see if he was breathing.

"He's breathing!" yelled Sid. "Take him to the doctor."

Two other station workers picked Jeff up and carried him away.

Sid's friend and fellow station worker Charley Hood walked around and examined the caboose. They immediately noticed the cash and coins were missing from the trunks as light came through the bullet holes in the walls.

"What do you think happened?" asked Charley.

"Robbery, but by who I don't know. If I was here, I would have stopped it," Sid answered confidently.

"What do you want to be – Sheriff one day?" Charley laughed.

"I don't know what I want to do with my life," Sid responded.

Just then, their boss, Alex Cane walked in through the back door. At the same moment the door connecting the caboose to the next car opened. The two young guards entered with their heads down.

"How could you let this happen?" yelled Alex. "Who robbed this train?" he demanded.

The two guards said nothing instead they just kept their heads down and wept. Alex slapped them both across the face and growled, "You're both fired."

The two guards ran out of the caboose not to be seen again.

"What's the plan then boss?" asked Sid.

"We'll need to get a message to Sheriff Frank Murphy of Pima County to step in and help," Alex responded.

Within the next hour, Alex, had telegraphed the Sheriff who promptly responded:

Organize a posse and capture them, keep ten percent of the cash findings for yourself and your men. I give you the authority to deputize your men.

Alex was happy to help, after all, if he captured them and the money, he'd make more money than he would in the whole year.

The next day, Alex organized Sid, Charley, and two other men, Don and Bruce to help. Armed with shotguns, revolvers, plenty of ammo, food and water, the men were prepared for a long journey. Alex learned that Jeff was still alive but would need some time to recover. He also discovered that two of the men had been shot; one badly and the name of the leader of the gang was Burt Alvord.

"Where do we start?" Sid asked Alex.

"Well, I suppose it's best to first head toward Willcox since that's where Burt was Constable," said Alex.

"Wait, hold on. Wouldn't it be smarter to follow the railroad tracks and go to the scene of the crime? There's a lot of blood-filled whiskey on the ground. If we go to the scene of the crime, we will most likely find a dried-up blood trail," Sid argued.

Alex knew Sid was right but made it seem like that was his idea all along. "Yes, that's what I meant, follow the tracks first and I bet the blood runs toward Willcox," Alex agreed.

The five men rode off. They spotted drops of dried-up blood along the tracks, but what they wanted to see was a lot of blood, and a trail that leading away from the tracks.

"Here!" yelled Charley as he pointed.

The blood was followed by hoofprints to the east toward a ridge of mountains in the opposite direction of Willcox. Sid stared at Alex and shook his head. This renewed the men's confidence and reassured Sid that he knew more than Alex. Because of his youth, he kept his mouth shut and let Alex take lead. Now that they were hot on the Alvord Gang's trail, they figured that they were only a couple of days behind them.

"Let's gain some ground men!" yelled Alex.

At the same time, the men raced their horses following the horse tracks. After a few miles, Alex abruptly stopped in front of a burnt-up cactus. Sid stopped to see what he was looking at. To his surprise, not only was there a burnt cactus, but there was a man sitting up against it with bloodstains covering his shirt. He looked dehydrated with his chapped lips.

Alex pointed his gun at the individual and demanded, "State your name."

The man coughed and struggled to speak. He held up his hand which was missing two fingers and was able to clearly say, "Jack."

Alex got off his horse, grabbed his water canteen, and helped Jack to some water.

"Ahh," said Jack, "thank you."

"Where are you hit?" asked Alex.

Jack pointed to his chest and coughed once more, this time spitting out blood.

Alex grabbed a piece of cloth from his saddlebag and offered it to Jack who cleaned off his face. "Tell me where your gang went, and we'll see to it that you get to a doctor," said Alex.

Jack hesitated, but then his eyes filled with rage. "They left me for dead last night," he said with every ounce of energy he had. He then pointed to the ridge of mountains in the distance.

"Tell me all their names," demanded Alex.

Jack coughed again letting out even more blood. "George and Louis Owens, Bob Brown, Bravo Juan Yoas, and that son of bitch, Burt Alvord who left me for dead," Jack spit. He forgot to mention Billy Stiles.

"Thank you," Alex said. He then turned toward Charley and instructed, "You take Jack to the doctor and we'll go on ahead and find the gang."

While Alex's back was turned, Jack slowly reached for his holster, pulled out his gun, and then aimed it at Alex. The sound of the gun cocking caused Alex to turn.

Without hesitation, Sid pulled out his gun and shot Jack in the chest, killing him instantly. Sid blew the smoke as it flowed out of the barrel, and then returned the gun back to its holster. Alex stood in shock, his mouth hanging open.

"Never trust an outlaw," said Sid.

"I'm calling you *Sid the Kid* from now on," Charley stated with a smile.

The men left Jack's body and proceeded onward. A few hours later, they reached the mountains. The tracks were now gone, and it was getting dark. They decided to make camp for the night and prepare for a potential long day tomorrow.

The sun rose the next day, and the men looked for any sign of the Alvord Gang. With no luck, Alex decided they were better off splitting into two groups than sticking together. Sid disagreed, thinking they were putting themselves in a weak position if one of them got caught. However, Sid listened to Alex, and he left with Charley in one group, while Alex, Don, and Bruce went in another direction. They decided to meet up on the other side of the mountain, however long it took.

After about thirty minutes of riding, Sid noticed an object resting on a rock ahead. He and Charley approached and noticed that it was an empty can of beans. Sid jumped off his horse, and felt the inside of the can. "It's still wet, they must be close," said Sid.

They left the can and continued; this time much more alert.

As they made the turn around the mountain, they knew that soon they'd meet back up with the others. However, Sid and Charley could hear yelling in the distance.

"What's that noise?" asked Charley.

"Yes, I hear it too," said Sid.

They got down off their horses, grabbed shotguns, and walked slowly as the noise got louder and louder. Sid was the first to see a few men standing close to each other. He sank to his knees and pulled Charley down and said, "Shh," with his finger to his lips. They held their shotguns and listened.

"I don't want to have to tell you again, put your guns down and we won't shoot ya," yelled Alex.

The response surprised Sid and Charley. "Your outlawing days are up, put your guns down!" Alex ordered.

Alex had somehow found the Alvord Gang before them. Alex, Bruce, and Don stood with their guns aimed at the six outlaws: Burt, Billy, Bravo, Bob, George and Louis.

"You're outnumbered sir. Look I don't have time for this," Burt called. He then turned to his men and said, "On the count of three shoot them."

"Oh no, we have to do something," Sid whispered to Charley.

"One," said Burt.

"Come on Charley, stand up with me," said Sid.

"Two," said Burt.

With all six Alvord Gang members backs facing them, Sid yelled, "Don't move." This froze and shocked the gang. "Drop the guns and on your knees or else all ten of us won't shoot."

None of the Alvord Gang members turned. Instead, they awaited instructions from Burt.

Sid grew impatient and had to make sure his lie was not exposed. Sid yelled again, "Okay men; shoot on the count of three – one, two ..." Before he could say three, Burt dropped his gun and went to his knees. His men followed suit. Alex and the two men quickly grabbed their guns while Sid and Charley tied the men's hands behind their backs.

Alex, Bruce, and Don then grabbed the bags of stolen cash and coins, and tied them onto their horses.

Burt looked behind him and laughed, "Good one kid!"

Billy and the rest of the men looked behind them as well seeing only Sid and Charley. They were first embarrassed, and then upset.

Alex and his men led the Alvord Gang across the desert, and back to Fairbank, where they were held in the local jail. The jail visit was short-lived, for that same day they were put on a train to Yuma. Sheriff Frank

Murphy had dispatched orders to send the gang to Yuma County where they'd be held in the Yuma Prison to await trial.

For the rest of his life, Alex bragged about how he had captured the gang. He enjoyed his newfound wealth while Sid remained humble and vowed to one day become Sheriff. After the taste of victory, Sid knew that his future was clear.

13: YUMA PRISON

The information that Three Fingered Jack gave to Alex Parsons was evidence enough to land all the men in prison, not to mention the money that was recovered. Despite the evidence, Burt pleaded his innocence, suggesting there wasn't enough evidence to support him and his gang being thrown in prison. Though Billy Stiles was present with Burt and the gang when they were captured, Jack had not mentioned him when he told Alex the names of those who were involved. Billy was able to work out a deal, paying only a fine of $100 which he happily did.

The judge was only going to give the rest of the men a two-year sentence, but after receiving a handwritten note from Jeff Milton stating that Alvord and his gang were responsible for not only the train robbery, but cattle rustling as well, that the judge decided to give each member a five-year sentence. Billy was the only man to avoid prison time.

On a hot day in early April 1900, Yuma Prison became home for Burt, Bob, Bravo, George, and Louis. What made the Yuma Prison so unique was that the jail cells were made of rock. A steel door was the only way in and out of each cell. Burt and Bob shared a cell, George was with his brother Louis, and Bravo shared a cell with a man by the name of Bill Downing. While the prison cells provided some necessary relief from the sun, they lacked ventilation. This made prison life rough, forcing the men to spend as much time as possible outside their cells in the heat where they could at least feel the wind. Despite this, prison life was not as tough as Burt had thought it would be. The prison housed a library, and the men were fixed with three small meals a day.

The prison was run by Mr. George Bravin, known as "The Warden." He was a man from Great Britain who maintained his English accent. He was always clean shaven, wore glasses, and constantly cleaned his gun. Respect was earned by the prisoners by the way he treated them, even the most hard-nosed. The Warden had a philosophy of befriending the inmates, but would shoot them in the back if they tried any funny business.

The men were resting in the shade on the prison grounds when The Warden approached and asked, "How are you boys adjusting?"

None of the men spoke but Burt, but he avoided the question. "Are we allowed to have visitors?"

"Well of course, every Sunday for thirty minutes someone can visit with you," The Warden answered. He then pointed in the opposite direction opposite from where they were toward a large, cast-iron gate which served as the entrance and exit to the prison. "That's where you can meet."

Burt nodded and said, "Understand."

"Anything I can get you boys? Food, water?" The Warden asked.

"Were good, I eat more here in one day than in three back home," said George Owens with a mouth full of bread.

The Warden tipped his cap, and then looked off in the distance again toward the gate where two men stood outside of the prison peering in. He walked over to see who it was while Burt used this opportunity to speak to his gang.

"Alright, I know this place doesn't seem all that bad, but I'm planning our escape. Our best shot is Billy," said Burt.

Just then the men heard a whistle and turned around. It was from George who then yelled, "Burt, come over here please."

Burt slowly walked over. He tried to see who George was talking to by screening the sun with his hands above his eyes. It was not until he got to the gate that he recognized one of the men. It was Jeff Milton wearing a cloth sling holding up his right arm. Jeff stared at Burt with an intense look, while Burt equally shared his look.

"Burt, these two men want to speak to you," said George.

"Well, I refuse to speak," said Burt.

The man who was with Jeff said, "You claim your innocence. If you are innocent then Jeff here is a liar. I will give you thirty seconds to prove Jeff is a liar and if you do, I will let you out."

Burt frowned and asked, "And who might you be?"

"Sheriff Frank Murphy," the man said touching his Silver Star badge on his vest.

"For a sheriff, you don't have much for brains. A good sheriff knows that what you just told me ain't legal. Only a judge can let me out, and I'm not talking," Burt then spit on the ground, turned, and walked back to his gang. Burt mumbled, "Let me out, oh, I will get out."

"What happened boss?" asked Bravo.

Burt addressed the gang, even Bill Downing who was unofficially resting with them, "Don't get too comfortable here." Burt slapped the bread out of George Owens hand. "We will get out of here at some point; just give me time to form a plan." That same night, Burt tossed and turned in his cot "No, no, no!" Burt yelled in his sleep waking Bob. Burt was laying in his bed throwing punches and kicks. Bob thought he was throwing a tantrum, something a kid would do. Then Burt woke up breathing heavily with his shirt soaked.

"What's wrong with you?" asked Bob.

"Bad … dreams," Burt had trouble explaining.

"Well, if this is what I'm going to be dealing with every night they might as well hang me now," said Bob.

Burt caught his breath, threw off his wet shirt and said, "No you idiot, I have very intense dreams sometimes, feel so real that it's hard to believe that I am not still actually dreaming."

Bob didn't know what say, so Burt continued. "I dream of being in gunfights, becoming very wealthy after robberies, and escaping prison. There's always a man who points his gun at me during the dream, but I dodge it. Everything always ends with me speaking to man who calls himself Roosevelt, followed by me standing with a woman overlooking water."

"Sounds like something out of a fiction novel," said Bob.

"I suppose so," Burt responded.

* * *

Over the course of the next two months, Burt fell into a daily routine consisting of going to library and reading, reading, and reading more. While none of the men wanted to question Burt, the gang elected Bravo to ask him why he was reading so much.

"Boss? We want to know why you like to read so much?" asked Bravo.

"Well Bravo, my father was the justice of the peace and he taught me that I can fill my head with more knowledge than anyone if I just read every day," said Burt.

Burt then showed Bravo the title of the book he was currently reading.

"I can't read, nor write," said Bravo.

Burt shook his head in disappointment. "It says, *Construction of all Things*, and I just learned how steel doors are made, and how to carve wood."

"What are you trying to say, you want to build prison doors?" Bravo asked looking confused.

"No, so I know now how it operates; the screws are made of metal, rather than steel. That is how we can escape," Burt smiled.

Over the next few weeks, Burt laid out his plans. He was going to teach his men how to carve wood into makeshift screws, the same size that held up the steel cell doors. The metal screws holding the doors on their hinges would be replaced by the wood ones essentially throwing off the lock alignment because of its weight difference, meaning the locks would appear secured, but the door would still swing open and shut freely. They would need to do this slowly and methodically, replacing one screw at time so they wouldn't be caught. Once their job was completed, and all the screws replaced, they would simply open their jail cell doors when they were ready to escape.

The next problem they faced was getting out through the main gate. They could not just simply walk out. The only other exit was through The Warden's office. If they could somehow distract him long enough, they could walk right out. While Burt contemplated the right course of action, he realized he'd need to get Billy to aid them from the outside. After three months of nonstop carving wooden screws day after day, Burt felt it was time to write Billy. He had to write in code as his letter would most likely be read by The Warden prior to being mailed. The only way to tell Billy exactly what he needed to do was to use mirror writing.

He wrote:

Bring six horses this upcoming Sunday at midnight. Meet half-a-mile south from the prison toward the Colorado River. Bring guns, food, and water.

But he wrote it this way:

Bring six horses this upcoming Sunday at midnight. Meet half-a-mile south from the prison toward the Colorado River. Bring guns, food, and water.

As expected, the letter was taken to The Warden for approval; And he summoned Burt to his office. "What does this mean?" asked The Warden.

"When I was young, I was fascinated by Egyptian hieroglyphics. This is just a note that reads about my health and wellbeing to my friend back home," Burt explained lying through his teeth.

The Warden was not sure if Burt meant the gang member that got off free, but assumed so. He examined the note once more, decided not to question it any further and allowed it to be sent.

Sunday had arrived and the men were anxious. They questioned whether they could actually pull it off. Bill Downing had earned the men's respect, but Burt questioned if he would be just as trustworthy outside of prison. Nevertheless, the escape plan was set, and would go down at midnight. The wooden screws had replaced the metal ones.

The Warden assumed he'd locked the cell doors as he did every night. The men then waited in their cells for Burt to take the lead.

"How will we know when it's midnight?" Bob asked Burt as they waited in their jail cell.

"Don't you hear the bell in town every day at noon and every night at midnight? It has been going off for months," said Burt.

Bob shook his head.

"My gang is full of idiots," said Burt under his breath.

"What's that?" asked Bob.

"I said, I hope my gang is full of excitement, because once were out its back to business," Burt answered.

Burt then got up to make sure the cell door would open and shut, which it did. He and Bob waited patiently until the bell rang out in the distance indicating it was midnight. Burt immediately opened the cell door, looked to his left down the other row of cells where Bravo, Bill, George, and Louis's were and noticed that only one of the cell doors was opened – it was Bravo and Bill Downing's.

What's the matter? Burt thought to himself. Then he whispered to Bob, "Stay here."

Burt quickly walked over to George and Louis's cell. "Let's go!" Burt demanded in a whispered tone.

"Were not going boss," said Louis.

"You see, we find this life is better for us, more food than ever before, a life of peace," said George Owens.

Burt frowned and said, "You have both wasted my time, good riddance, and we'd better never cross paths again." Burt scoffed, and took off with Bravo, Bill, and Bob toward George Bravin's office. Once there, the men crouched down low on the side of the small wooden office building.

"What's the plan again boss?" asked Bravo.

"We need to get him outside for a minute so we can sneak in behind him. That's why I have these," Burt took a handful of dead brush and twigs along with a matchbox from his pants pockets. "I'm going to light a small fire at the prison entrance, and then when I come back here, I'll will throw a small rock at George's door. Hopefully he'll see the fire out the window and walk toward it. This will be our cue to escape through his office."

"Can we help boss?" asked Bob.

"If you want a job done right you do it yourself," said Burt.

Burt walked off quickly but quietly toward the entrance, lit the brush and twigs on fire, and then hustled back to the men. He crouched down, picked up a small pebble and threw it against the office door.

They immediately heard The Warden in the office. He opened the door slowly and looked out. Burt could see The Warden was in his pajamas but wasn't wearing his glasses, and his eye lids were half shut. He clearly did not notice the fire and closed the door.

"Are you serious?" questioned Burt.

The fire was almost out and Burt knew he only had one more try at this. He picked up another pebble and threw it harder against his door.

The Warden opened the door quickly this time, looked out, and this time Burt noticed he'd put his glasses on. The Warden's gun was drawn and he called, "Who's out there?" He looked to his right and seeing the small fire, ran toward it. As The Warden stomped on the ground trying to put the fire out, the gang made quick work of walking through the front door and out the back exiting the prison.

"Follow me!" Burt announced.

14: FUGITIVES

The gang ran together following Burt in the direction of the Colorado River. A whistle was heard in the distance which stopped the gang in their tracks. Burt immediately assumed it was Billy and told the men to push forward. It was not long before they heard horses in the same direction of the whistle giving the men a sigh of relief that the plan had worked. When they finally reached the horses, the men were out of breath and sweating. It was dark but they could make out a person sitting on one of the horses.

"Thanks Billy, you are my best friend after all," said Burt exhaling loudly.

To the men's surprise, the response came from a woman. "Thanks honey, I only do this sort of favor for my good friends."

"Kate?" Burt asked, puzzled but pleased.

"Best hurry now before you all get caught; you men are on your own. Billy wants you to meet him back in Tombstone. Don't take one step into my saloon, he said to meet him in one week at Burt's childhood home which is now abandoned," Kate instructed.

"How can we thank you?" asked Burt.

Kate jumped off her horse, went up to Burt and gave him a big kiss on the lips. "Go now!" yelled Kate.

Kate gently pushed Burt away, and without hesitation, the gang left Kate.

They arrived in Tombstone one week later. It was midday so they stayed on the outskirts of town waiting for it to get dark planning on not being seen. The plan was to meet up at Burt's childhood home. Thankfully, Burt's childhood home was away from the busy Fremont and Allen Street where all the main saloons and town shops were located. When it was dark enough the men made their way to the house, parked their horses in front, and Burt led them through the front door. To Burt, the house smelled different, almost of damp moss. In the middle of the room was Billy Stiles sitting on a chair surrounded by six empty chairs, a lantern, and a large bottle of whiskey sitting on the floor. "You men look like hell," Billy grinned.

Just then, Billy noticed the unknown member of the gang, Bill Downing. "Who are you, and where are George and Louis?" he asked.

"Bill Downing, sir," Bill responded.

"You got to be kidding me, another name starting with the letter B, and we basically have the same name. No, we're going to call you Downing," said Billy.

Burt, Bob, Bravo, and Downing sat down leaving two unoccupied chairs.

"George and Louis are not to be mentioned ever again, they stayed behind," said Burt before spitting on the ground.

"Okay Burt, you are all fugitives now. What do you think is the best course of action now, lay low for a while right?" asked Billy.

"Well Billy, first off thank you for sending Kate to do the job, smart move. Secondly, now is the time to hit the trains hard, we have an opportunity to get rich quick. I'll organize everything, but from now on we must cover our faces at all times …" Burt said before Billy interrupted.

"Why don't we just get out of this town, leave this county, and never return?" argued Billy.

Burt stood up with his hands on his hips. "I am the boss. Don't you think I've thought of that already? We will leave town and head south to Mexico. We'll live there and when necessary, cross the border to conduct business. Bravo, you gotta contact your connections in Mexico and get us a place to stay where we can develop a plan," Burt instructed.

Bravo nodded and said, "I already know where we can stay."

"You see Billy, it will all work out," Burt sat back down.

Billy felt he needed to save his own skin. He didn't want to end up in prison rotting away, or even worse hanged because he followed Burt's rules. He came up with a plan so that he would still be part of the gang, but not be in on the robberies. "What about me though? I'm the only free man here. Wouldn't I be a better asset if I stayed here? Be the one to take the cattle to auctions, get all the necessary supplies needed for a train robbery?" questioned Billy.

"You know Billy; you're a smart man. I never thought of that, we could really use you in that way. That's settled then. Now let's go break open the bottle of whiskey," responded Burt with a smile.

Burt grabbed the whiskey bottle, took one big gulp, and said, "Ahh! It has been way too long."

The men spent the next couple hours drinking and sharing stories of prison life with Billy. Burt was getting quite drunk. He slumped over in his chair and rested his eyes while the men continued their conversation.

"So, what's your story, you certainly dress fancy for an outlaw?" Billy asked Downing.

Downing was balding, had a long brown mustache, but Billy was referring to Downing's tan suit jacket. Downing placed both hands on his jacket and responded, "Took it off the man I killed. But if you're asking for my story, I'm from Texas, escaped capture by the Texas Rangers and relocated to Pearce where I was working at the Esperanza Ranch. That's where I learned the art of cattle rustling. I eventually moved to Willcox and ended up getting into a drunken argument with a man named Will Traynor and shot and killed him. That's what landed me in Yuma Prison. That Will fella was an idiot and claimed to be a Rough Rider with the now Governor of New York, Theodore Roosevelt."

Burt immediately woke up jolting which startled the men.

"Roosevelt?" Burt asked.

"Yep – the Governor of New York, why?"

Burt hesitated, looked at the gang and said, "No reason."

The awkward conversation was relieved by a knock at the door. All the men jumped up and pulled out their guns except Billy.

"Settle down men, it's just Kate," Billy said calmly.

Burt stumbled but managed to walk over and open the door.

"So, this is where that big bad fugitive Burt Alvord grew up," Kate laughed.

"Always nosey," said Burt.

Kate was holding baskets of food that was still warm. It was the leftovers from the saloon. The men did not care, and happily finished everything she brought.

"Thanks ma'am," said Bravo.

"Don't expect this kind of treatment going forward, but if you need anything just send a message. I just wanted to drop this off, now I best be leaving," Kate walked out the door.

Burt ran after her. "Wait!" Burt called.

"Yes honey?" Kate stopped.

Burt was slurring but knew what he wanted to say, "I ... um ... just needed to tell you. *Hiccup.* If I send you a note, it will be in mirror writing. *Hiccup.* Meaning when you get it you need to hold it up to a mirror to read it. *Hiccup.* And one more ... *hiccup* ... thing. I love you."

Kate paused and tried to figure out how to respond. She touched the side of his face, and then put her face up to close to his, and the smell of whiskey overtook her. "You're drunk, you don't love me."

"No ... *hiccup*. I do."

Kate started to walk away but said, "Tell me that when you're sober." She turned away but not before smiling.

Burt watched as she continued into the night. However, once she was out of sight he had a feeling that something wasn't right.

What's that smell? Burt thought to himself.

"Burt! We got a problem," shouted Billy from inside the house.

Burt walked in and stood there frozen watching flames as they started to engulf the room.

"What the hell happened?" asked Burt.

"Downing accidently kicked over the lantern. Get out!" shouted Bravo.

The men quickly exited and watched as the fire slowly took over the house.

"What are you waiting for, were fugitives, we need to get the hell out of here," Burt ordered.

The men, including Billy jumped on their horses and rode off. Billy went in a different direction leaving the gang. About ten minutes later, the men were a mile outside of town. They turned to look back toward Tombstone easily seeing the fire as it destroyed Burt's childhood home. Bob pulled his horse up next to Burt's and placed a hand on his shoulder as Burt let one, and only one tear roll down his cheek.

15: DUST

The Alvord Gang occupied a cotton farmhouse just outside Nogales across the border in Mexico. The house had been lent to them by a friend of Bravo's which consisted of horses, chickens, and fields of cotton as far as the eye could see. The men were responsible for taking care of the farm in exchange for living there. Burt knew he could not maintain the farm unless they had a staff of people, not just members of his gang to do the dirty work. As long as the farm was run well and brought in money, they would not be bothered by the Mexican government.

Burt employed several Mexicans to work the farm, and left the day-to-day operations to a man he'd once met many years ago – Francisco Nieves, while Burt and his gang plotted their next great robbery. Francisco lived in the area and had given up his life as an outlaw and was looking for a quieter life. Burt filled that void and in return Francisco was a loyal man and gave Burt a lot of good advice. Nieves wore overalls, and a wide-brimmed leather hat to block out the sun. His hat was so big that often the men could not see his eyes, which led to his nickname – *No Eyes Nieves*.

They were now living the good life. Burt's intentions were to keep robbing and retire young. Over the course of a few months, he and his gang had successfully robbed a handful of trains, never stealing from the passengers, but rather whatever just the cash that the train was transporting.

They were able to compile a large sum of cash valued at $50,000 over their robbing spree.

The event that would make them known throughout the West was when Burt and Billy faked their own deaths by putting a note on the caskets of two dead men stating that Burt Alvord and Billy Stiles had been killed by the hands of Jeff Milton. Once it was quickly discovered that the note was false and Jeff refuted the claim, Jeff more than ever wanted them captured.

Burt knew word would quickly get out about them so just as quickly as they began, they slowed down. It was time for the gang to take a different approach. Burt decided rather than robbing as a group they'd split into groups of two and his men would do the dirty work, not Burt. All the cash they accumulated was stashed in a large crate buried underneath the front porch of the farmhouse, hidden even from the most cunning of eyes.

One very windy day in January 1901 Burt directed Bob Brown and Bravo Juan Yoas to seize loot from the next train that rolled into Willcox. Bob and Bravo climbed onto their horses holding onto their hats before they could fly away.

"Are we to steal from the passengers?" Bob asked.

"No, we will never steal from passengers. There's always a safe located in the train conductor's compartment room near the front of the train. Instead of holding the man at gunpoint, pose as workers that have been directed to take the money to the bank. Cover your mouths with bandannas and keep your hats on so it will be difficult for someone to recognize you. Act confidently," Burt instructed.

Bravo's vest flapped in the wind. "No guns drawn, no shots to be fired then?" he asked.

Burt smiled, "Work on your acting skills on your ride up there. I'll see you both in two days' time – safe journey."

Bravo and Bob tipped their hats, still hold onto them with one hand, and rode off.

"I sure hope we don't get recognized," said Bob.

"Like Burt said, we'll cover our mouths," Bravo replied.

"Alright so how do you want to do this? You want to do all the talking?" asked Bob.

Bravo shook his head and replied, "We best just feed off of one another. If we practice lines like an actor, we won't sound truthful."

They rode much of the rest of the journey in silence until they spotted the train in the distance not far from stopping at the Willcox train station. As they reached the outskirts of town, the wind picked up even more at their backs. The wind threw dirt into the air making it tough to see. The air whistled as if mocking them for foolishly being there. Bravo turned to look behind him and saw trouble.

"Look!" Bravo yelled as he pointed.

"It's a dust storm! Quick we need to head to the station," Bob announced.

The dust storm was not far behind and closing in fast. Bob and Bravo forced their horses onward as quickly as they could. Their hats flew off their heads and out of sight without any warning. Both men crouched low and held onto their bridle straps and arrived at the station at the same moment the train stopped and they were engulfed by the dust storm.

Bob coughed, "I can't see."

Bravo covered his whole face with his bandanna, grabbed two empty bags for the cash, and then escorted Bob by the arm and said, "To the train car."

Train station workers who were outside ran into the station for cover to wait for it to pass. Bravo and Bob made it to the train conductor's car and knocked loudly. The conductor opened the door and helped them inside for protection. While Bravo lowered his bandanna to only cover his mouth, Bob still had not donned his.

"What a storm," said the train conductor.

"You got that right," replied Bob.

Bravo grabbed Bob's bandanna out of his own pocket and placed it in his hand. Bob's face grew red, and he quickly put it on covering his mouth.

The train conductor looked at Bob curiously and said, "Can I help you men with something?"

"Sorry to bother you sir but we're here to take the money in the safe to the bank," said Bravo.

"Oh yeah – I thought this cash was going to Pearce. Who authorized this?" the man asked.

Bravo paused and looked at Bob. "Well … umm …," Bravo started but was then interrupted by Bob.

"U.S. Marshal Jeff Milton, sir," said Bob confidently.

"Jeff? Huh, I don't know any Jeff," the conductor looked at him suspiciously.

"Look sir, we're just here to do our job. I can't bring Jeff here to prove it with this storm," said Bravo.

The train conductor looked out the window and said, "Yes, I suppose this is a bad one." He then turned and twisted the lock combination of the safe. The lock clicked with every correct number the train conductor landed on as Bravo handed one of the bags to Bob. Above the train conductor's head was a Wanted Sign. It stated:

WANTED: Burt Alvord $10,000 Dead or Alive,

and $5,000 a Gang Member Dead or Alive

Just as he finished reading, the train conductor opened the safe and began placing the cash into the bags that grew larger with the quantity. Just then, with only a few stacks of bills left, the door opened and a teenage man entered.

"Wow, what a dust storm out there," the kid said brushing dust off his clothes. He then looked around to see what was going on. "What's happening here?" he asked.

"Oh, these two men work for the U.S. Marshal. They're taking the cash to the bank. What can I help you with Sid?" asked the train conductor.

Sid frowned, and scratched his head before asking Bravo and Bob, "What are your names?"

"I'm Billy Burts and this here is Will Brooks," Bob said as the conductor finished putting the rest of the cash into the bags.

"Curious, I don't think I have seen you two men around here before," Sid said.

"Were from Texas, just got into town to do this job," said Bravo.

"We best be going, this storm is not going to stop us," Bob started to move away.

Bob and Bravo began walking toward the door but then Bob tripped over a loose floorboard causing his bandanna to slide down revealing his face. He quickly dropped the bag of cash, pulled the bandanna back up, but not before Sid got a good look at him. Sid bent down and grabbed the bag of cash and Bob froze. His heart pounded and his palms started sweating.

"Don't forget your bag," said Sid.

Bob grabbed the bag and took a deep breath, then laughed awkwardly, "Thank you sir, good day."

Bob was first out followed by Bravo. They shut the door and ran to their horses. The dust storm was still raging making visibility almost impossible. They climbed onto their horses and Bravo yelled, "This way!" They placed their bandannas up over their eyes, and once again forced their horses onward. As they got past the train station, they heard a man yelling something. Bravo kept his head down as Bob turned back to see who was yelling. The wind quieted for a moment and the voice was clear for only a moment.

"Stop those men! They stole the cash," the voice yelled.

However, the dust storm was still too violent for anyone to go after them. Bravo and Bob escaped capture and got away with all the cash. The amount to be counted later. Around a mile later, the dust storm passed and they were in the clear.

"You gave us away," said Bravo.

"How?" asked Bob.

"Billy Burts. You couldn't think of anything else?" Bravo said with disgust.

"Look we have the cash, let's not tell the boss about this. He has been drinking heavily again and we don't want to make him angry," said Bob.

"Agreed," replied Bravo.

16: EL PELUDO

Bravo and Bob made it back to the farmhouse to find Burt drunk. He was smiling over a letter from Kate before kissing it, then folding it into his pocket. Burt didn't notice that both men were missing their hats. Instead, Bob could see Burt was not well rested and had dark bags under his eyes. Bob recognized the look from their days at Yuma Prison the day after Burt had those dream terrors. An unknown man sat in the room with Burt and Downing. Before Bravo and Bob could present their treasure, Burt announced, "This is Augustine Chacon, the newest member of our gang." He was a large man, with a heaver build than Burt and had a thick, long brown beard.

"Welcome," said Bravo.

Burt stumbled to get up out of his chair. A nearly empty small whiskey bottle sat on the table next to him. "How did it go?" asked Burt.

Bravo and Bob emptied their bags of cash out onto the table knocking the whiskey bottle onto the ground. Burt ignored the bottle, as his eyes lit up seeing all the loot. He grabbed a hand full of cash astonished by what he was seeing. "How?" asked Burt.

"A massive dust storm allowed us to go undetected," replied Bravo.

"And no one saw you?" asked Burt.

"Just the train conductor, he handed the cash over to us. No one else," Bob grinned nervously.

Burt grabbed even more cash and said, "There must be at least $20,000 here!"

"It looks like we won't need to steal anything for a while. In fact, we should probably lay low. There was a reward for capture sign for us – $10,000 for you Burt, and $5,000 for each of us," Bob handed Burt the reward sign on a folded piece of paper.

Burt crumpled up the paper and stepped on it. "Ha, why slow down now?" He then picked the whiskey bottle up from the floor and held it in the air and said, "Tonight we celebrate, tomorrow we get even richer."

Downing picked up the WANTED sign and walked over to throw it in the trash bin. He then hesitated for a moment, scratched his head, and stuffed it into his pants pocket unnoticed by the men. He turned back around and joined back up with them. That night the men partied, singing songs, and drinking heavily. Bravo and Bob had an opportunity to learn more about Chacon's background. He bragged about how many people he'd killed, and joked about how Burt once tried to chase him down after a bank robbery in Bisbee, but could never find him. His openness to talk about the murders alarmed Bravo and Bob.

If he kills everyone he doesn't like, then it won't be long before we're next, thought Bob.

Downing spent much of the night reading the newspaper, which he claimed he'd been given inadvertently the last time he was across the border weeks ago.

"Look here boys, it says the Arizona Rangers have been established, and their first order of business is to clamp down on the border."

Burt scoffed and scratched his bald head. "Don't bother me … *hiccup*." He looked at the money again. "It seems to me that we are the smartest outlaws in the West."

"The Arizona Rangers will be well trained, and will be in many numbers," said Downing.

Chacon laughed and said in a low voice, "Ain't no Rangers going to stop me."

After a long night of drinking, the farm's one and only rooster announced the sun was rising. None of the men woke up or even moved, except Chacon. He enjoyed waking at dawn and getting a good day's work in. He strapped on his boots, but on his hat, and went to aid the farmworkers for the day.

Hours later, Burt and the rest of the gang finally awoke.

"No night terrors or visions?" Bob asked Burt.

"Seems like the more I drink, the less I dream," replied Burt as he got up and walked to the window overlooking the farm. He noticed Chacon holding up large bags of cotton. "Now that's why I welcomed him into this gang. You men ought to learn what hard work looks like. That's a man who earns his respect," Burt said. He then paused before looking at Downing. "Speaking of respect, you Downing, it's your turn to earn my respect. Bravo and Bob brought in all this money. Today, you and Chacon will ride to Tombstone and rob the bank. And before you say anything, thinking it will be impossible, know that Billy and Kate will assist."

"But the Rangers," worried Downing.

"They don't know you, let alone that you're in this gang. Just like Bravo and Bob, cover your faces," said Burt.

"So, what's the plan?"

"There's supposed be a new shipment of cash delivered by horse and carriage in three days. Billy and Kate will go into the bank to discuss a new loan for a saloon with the owner at the same time that the delivery is scheduled. While the owner is distracted, hold the delivery man at gunpoint, steal the cash, and leave. No gunfighting, no blood spilled. I expect you to explain every word of this to Chacon on your journey north," Burt ordered.

Burt then opened the backdoor and looking at Chacon, he yelled, "It's time to get rich!"

Chacon dropped his bags of cotton and smiled. An hour later, Downing and Chacon readied their horses, cleaned their guns, and prepared their bags with food and water. They rode off in the mid-afternoon headed toward Tombstone.

"What's the plan?" Chacon asked Downing.

"Bank robbery. We're going to hold the delivery man at gunpoint, and leave with no blood spilled," said Downing.

"Well, that's no fun. What's a robbery without spilled blood?" questioned Chacon.

"That's what the boss said," said Downing.

The two men rode on and camped out for two days, and on the third they made their way to Tombstone. Before they got into town, they passed by the Boothill Graveyard. Chacon laughed, "Sent many men in there." The comment alarmed Downing a bit. He started to believe all the stories he was telling a few days ago about killing men. Despite Chacon's words, Downing had a job to do, and an opportunity to show Burt he was worthy of being in the gang.

As they made their way into town, Downing told Chacon to cover his face with a bandanna. They rode their horses past the front entrance of the bank and noticed both Billy and Kate sitting on a bench outside. Neither party acknowledged one another but both were aware each other's presence. Downing and Chacon slipped to the back of the bank building where they waited. As they did, Downing pulled a piece of paper from his pocket, crumpled it up, and threw it on the ground.

"What are you doing?" asked Chacon.

"Getting rid of trash," Downing responded.

"Whatever," Chacon responded.

Moments later, a wagon pulled up next to them behind the bank. Downing got down off his horse and peered inside the bank window. He could now see Billy and Kate standing inside but not talking to anyone. He waited for what was just seconds, but to him felt like an hour. His patience wore thin, so he told himself to get things started. The man in the wagon had his head buried inside a large box in the very back. Downing secured his bandanna, pulled out his gun, and pointed it at the man.

"Hands up!" Downing announced.

Chacon did nothing but watch. He had held many people at gunpoint throughout his life and enjoyed the show. The man pulled his head outside the box and turned to face Downing.

"What do you want? I don't have anything of value to you," said the man.

"All the money. Now!" Downing ordered.

"What money?" the man asked.

Downing then pushed the man away and looked inside the box. It was not money, but blocks of ice.

"Ice?" Downing questioned.

Chacon pulled his bandanna down and laughed, but as Downing was looking inside the box another wagon pulled up manned by two men, one young and clean shaven, and the other older with a short white beard. They stopped next to the awkward scene wondering what was happening.

Chacon asked the two men, "You the men with the bank loot?"

"Depends on who's asking," replied the younger man.

Chacon proceeded to pull out his gun, and fired two shots, hitting both men in the gut. They dropped off the wagon bench and landed on the ground bleeding. The man with the ice box wagon ran off.

"Hurry! We only have about twenty seconds," said Downing.

Downing scrambled to the back of the wagon, opened up a small crate, the only one that was present. He grabbed two hands full of cash and ran to his horse. As he climbed onto his horse, the door to the back of the bank opened. It was the owner, armed with a shotgun. Chacon immediately fired at the bank owner, missing him above the shoulder. The bank owner fired back missing Chacon as the shot went over his head. Chacon then jumped off his horse at the same time that the bank owner hid behind the backdoor. Suddenly, Downing and Chacon heard a loud thud. It was the bank owner being dragged inside the building by Billy.

"What are you doing?" demanded the bank owner.

"Saving your life!" Billy yelled.

Kate looked out the window to see Downing and Chacon riding away; then looked down and saw the two men bleeding on the ground. She ran outside to tend to the men, followed by the bank owner and Billy.

"You let them get away," said the bank owner.

"You'd be dead if it wasn't for me," responded Billy.

"They're dead," said Kate checking the men's pulses.

"Can't believe he robbed me again," complained the bank owner.

"Who?" asked Billy.

"That man with the large beard, he's known as *El Peludo*, and is known for killing many men. I'm not sure who the other man was, his face was covered," said the bank owner.

Just then the bank owner took a step backward and kicked something. He looked down and spotted a piece of paper. He bent down, picked it up, and unfolded and read it to himself. He clenched it tightly before saying, "We got a problem."

17: MANHUNT

"What does it say?" asked Kate.

"Information for the U.S. Marshal that I heard is in town. You two ought to head out, we can discuss your loan another day," the bank owner said dismissing them.

A handful of Tombstone citizens helped carry the two dead men away as Kate and Billy started to leave. Billy turned around one last time and noticed that the bank owner had thrown the piece of paper on the ground and went inside the building.

"Hold on, Kate," said Billy.

He ran back over and grabbed the paper slipping it into his pocket and then caught up with Kate. They both made their way into Kate's saloon where around ten men were sitting around drinking and playing cards. Behind Kate and Billy a man with a long, brown mustache entered and immediately walked toward one of the tables where three men were playing cards. As he passed Billy, he gave him a curious look as if he knew him. However, he did not stop and went over to the three men.

"That's Jeff Milton," Billy whispered to Kate.

"Quick now. I smell trouble. What does that paper say?" asked Kate.

They went over to the bar and sat down. Billy pulled out the paper, unfolded and read out an address located in Mexico, followed by: "*Robbery courtesy of the Burt Alvord Gang. If you capture them, I want the reward and my freedom. Bill Downing.*"

"Oh no. I bet that Jeff Milton is enlisting those men to go capture him," said Kate.

Billy turned just in time to see Jeff and the three men get up and make their way to the exit. "I bet you're right," said Billy.

Billy worried that if the gang was captured it would lead to his involvement in the bank robbery. In a matter of seconds, he contemplated leaving town or going to Burt's aid. "I don't know what to do," Billy stated.

"What feels right?" asked Kate.

"I want to leave the West altogether but something keeps pulling me back," Billy answered.

"That's your conscious. If I could leave to save him I would, but I'm no match for four lawmen. You go try to save him, and if you all get captured, send me a message about your next escape plan," said Kate with a smile.

Billy nodded slowly, and then Kate poured him a shot of whiskey. He threw it back, stood up, and walked out to go alert Burt hopefully before Jeff and his men arrived. Billy hopped on his horse and bolted out of Tombstone toward Mexico without any food or water other than what little he already had in his bag. Billy knew it was a three-day ride and he needed to push his horse, with little breaks to get there first.

Meanwhile, Jeff and the three men, armed with plenty of ammo and guns raced south to Mexico as well. The men Jeff enlisted were John, Henry, and Paul, all relatively young, in their early twenties, but well led by Jeff. They rode nonstop for twelve hours before resting in the middle of the night. "We need to stop now men, we don't want to tire out our horses too much or we'll be walking there," said Jeff.

On the third day, Billy had a slight lead on Jeff and his men with both parties not more than two miles out from the farmhouse. Billy was exhausted, and to make matters worse there seemed to be something wrong with his horse. The horse was foaming at the mouth and had begun to slow down. Billy thought the horse was about to fall so he leapt off and rolled in the dirt narrowly missing being pinned to the ground by the horse's weight. Billy got up gingerly but was okay. The horse was still breathing but was clearly in great pain. Billy pulled out his gun, pointed at the horse's head and shot one bullet ending the poor animal's misery. Billy then placed the gun back into its holster then put his hands on top of his head. He felt dizzy and light-headed and he dropped to both knees. Just as he landed, he heard the stampede of hoofbeats in the near distance. *Oh, my I must be losing my mind,* he thought. He looked around but could not see anything, nothing looked clear; not until he saw a large blurry image in front of him.

"Need help sir?" asked a man.

Billy rubbed his eyes just as a water canteen landed on the ground in front of him.

"Thank you, sir," said Billy.

The water brought him back to life a little bit, and his vision cleared somewhat. He rubbed his eyes once more and saw the sight he wished he hadn't seen; it was Jeff Milton and the three men.

"Billy Stiles, what are you doing here?" asked Jeff.

"Paying a visit to an old friend; what's your business here?" asked Billy.

"I'm paying your friend a visit myself. On men!" yelled Jeff who left Billy in the dust as they barreled on to the farmhouse.

No, thought Billy. He kept the canteen in hand and ran after them following their tracks. He ran as fast as he could quickly filling his clothes with sweat. As he got near the farmhouse, he could see in the distance as Jeff and the men circled the property and what appeared to be a dead man lying face down in front of the house. As Billy drew even closer within 100 feet of the property, Jeff confronted him.

"Where are they?" asked Jeff.

"What? How would I know? Who's dead?" Billy replied.

Billy looked behind Jeff and his horse and saw that it was Bill Downing lying face down in a pool of blood.

"Seems to me you're in on this, and you are going to tell me where they are," said Jeff.

Just then, John, one of Jeff's men approached holding a man's shoulder and forcing him toward them as he held a gun at his back.

"State your name?" demanded Jeff.

"They call me Francisco Nieves, and I run this farm," he answered.

"Don't lie to us. You see that dead man over there. Where is Burt Alvord?" Jeff growled.

Nieves paused, crossed his arms, and said nothing. Jeff got off his horse, pulled out his gun and now not only did Nieves have a gun at his back, there was also one pointed at his chest.

"I don't have all day," said Jeff.

Just then John pointed in the distance and said, "Look."

The men turned and spotted four men walking in front of two other men on horseback. Billy stepped back unsure of what was about to happen. Jeff's men gripped their guns ready for a gunfight. But as the men walked forward it became clear who they were. It was Burt, Bob, Chacon, and Bravo with their hands tied in front of their body. Jeff and his men kept their guns up in case they were being played. The two men on horseback held no guns, but instead grinned.

"These men are yours Marshal," said one of the men.

"And who do I owe this too?" asked Jeff.

"The name is *Sid the Kid,* and this here is Charley. We captured them once before, but this manhunt was even sweeter the second time. They revealed their identities when that moron Bravo," he pointed at him, "showed his face while robbing a train. We followed their tracks here. Being that we've done all this work I expect we'll be receiving the reward," Sid said holding Burt's gun up as a trophy.

Jeff lowered his gun signaling to his men to do the same. "Thanks kid, you'll be rewarded for this. It's back to prison for these fools, if they're not hung first," said Jeff. He then turned to John and said, "Grab Billy, he's in on this, too."

Billy put up no fight, he felt numb as John escorted him over to Burt and his gang. While Bob, Chacon, and Bravo hung their heads in embarrassment, Burt eyes filled with hate glared at Jeff but he said nothing.

18: POTION

Burt woke up coughing in the middle of a cold night in December 1901. He and his gang had been thrown back into Yuma Prison many months ago, and were again George Bravin's responsibility. Burt continued to cough throughout the night unable to sleep, and whenever he attempted to lie down his head hurt. It was one of the coldest nights he could remember. George Bravin had been mortified and nearly lost his job when Burt and his gang escaped. He received a second chance that he never thought he would get. In an attempt to minimize the gang's contact with one another, for fear of them plotting another escape, George limited their outside time from what had been four hours a day before down to one, and kept them in separate cells. Burt was clearly sick, and the next day he pleaded with George to get him a doctor. George agreed and said the doctors would see him later that day.

The afternoon did not provide much warmth either. The rock-lined prison cell walls seemed to trap the cold just like the heat for much of the year. Burt reclined on his bed, weak and coughing. When he heard keys rattling outside his cell door, Burt kept his eyes closed as the sound of footsteps approached the door.

"I am Doctor John Walter, how are you feeling Burt?" the man asked.

Burt kept his eyes closed and responded, "Are you a saphead? I'm as sick as a horse."

John felt Burt's forehead and looked at him intently and said, "I can see that you're not okay, you are very warm, and it is pretty cold outside. I am going to request that you be sent to the hospital tonight." He then walked out of the cell where George was waiting.

Burt could not hear what was being said but he George sounded very upset. The doctor walked back into the cell with George.

"George and I are going to carry you out to my wagon Burt," the doctor explained.

"Are you kidding?" asked George. "He is bigger than the both of us; we're going to need more men."

George exited the cell and whistled while pointing at two inmates who were outside their cell. Both men hustled over and followed George into the cell.

"Both you men grab a leg while we grab his arms. We're taking him to the doctor's wagon," George ordered.

As Burt was being lifted, he opened his eyes for a moment to see who was holding his legs. It was George and Louis Owens. Burt shook his head and uttered, "Kill me now," before closing his eyes once more not awakening until the next morning.

Burt awoke to see three other beds filled with men sleeping, followed by a Native American man sitting at a desk, writing. He could not have been more than twenty years old, wore glasses, and not a whisker on his face. Glass bottles mostly filled with liquid sat on the desk along with an unlit candle. Burt was more conscious than the night before but now had a runny nose and a headache.

"Where's the doctor?" asked Burt.

The man turned and said, "That is me, I'm Doctor John." He then stood and walked over to Burt holding up one of his small half-filled bottles with a light brown liquid. "Looks like you made it through the night, you had me worried there for a bit." The doctor started to hand Burt the bottle, but just as Burt reached out to take it, he realized that he could barely move his left arm. He looked down to see his wrist handcuffed to the bed. Burt was forced to grab the bottle with his right hand which was free.

"Take a sip of this," the doctor instructed.

Even though his nose was clogged the smell was strong enough for Burt to make out the odor of old eggs, coffee beans, and whiskey. He frowned and asked, "What is it?"

"It's an old Yuma Indian Tribe potion. I can't tell you what's in it for it's a secret," he said with a smile.

Burt frowned again, and examined the potion. He swirled it around and noticed it was rather thick. The size of the bottle itself looked like it belonged to a baby. He looked at the doctor who was still smiling, then took a deep breath before taking a small sip of the potion. Burt almost threw up but managed to keep it down.

"There you go!" the doctor said. "Now you should be back to yourself in no time. But if you barf it up stay away from the candles, this stuff is highly flammable." He then took the bottle and walked away.

Burt wondered if he had just been poisoned. But then his thoughts focused on the word flammable. And as his headache started to recede, and one nostril opened up, his mind began racing with ideas and thoughts about how he could escape prison.

"Hey doctor? That crazy potion of yours seems to be working. Do you think I can have a couple bottles of that in case I need more or for the other prisoners?"

"You liked it huh? Sure, you can have four bottles for $10."

"$10? How can I pay for it, I have no money on me?" Burt complained.

"That's my price," the doctor responded crossing his arms.

Just then one of the men on the other beds sat up. He was older man with a sling around his arm. "That's a fair price for that potion," said the man.

"But I got no money," said Burt.

"Hey, I know who you are. You are that outlaw fellow, Alvord, right?" the old man's eyes lit up. Burt nodded in response. "You must be worth a lot of money." He then turned to the doc, "You should have asked for more money; he is a rich man."

"I told you I ain't got no money," Burt was now annoyed.

"Don't you have someone who can bring your money?" asked the man.

Burt thought about that for a moment and then a light bulb went off. *Kate*, he thought to himself. He then announced, "Yes, I do actually. How about I send a letter to my contact and ask them to send the money to you? I will take the potions with me now and the money should be here in a few weeks."

"You see, there is a lot of demand right now for this potion. Practically everyone around town needs it. This is going to cost you more, $20 for the lot," the doctor stated.

"$20?" Burt questioned. He then paused and contained himself from attacking the doctor for playing him. "$20 it is then," he said calmly. Burt then reached out and signaled for the doc to hand over the bottles.

"No, no money here, no potions. Pay me first then I'll send them to you."

"Agreed," said Burt who then grabbed his throat. "Doctor? My throat is starting to hurt now; I think I need another sip of that potion."

"Sure thing," the doc handed the bottle back to Burt.

Just then a loud knock thudded against the door.

"Coming," yelled the doctor who proceeded to open the door.

Burt kept the cap on the bottle and quickly placed it in his pants pocket hoping no one would notice. As he looked up, he noticed that the old man had seen what he'd done. Burt placed his finger to lips and whispered, "I'll make you a rich man if you say nothing, what's your name?"

"I am an old man; I don't need no money. What I want is the scamper juice. My name is Fred," he whispered back.

"Scamper juice?" Burt wondered aloud.

"You know, whiskey. That's what us old timers call it," Fred grinned.

"No problem. I will have a big bottle sent to you in two weeks' time," said Burt.

Fred smiled but then grabbed his chest. His face grew pale.

"Are you okay?" asked Burt.

The doctor had opened the door and George Bravin entered to take Burt back to the prison.

"Doctor, you ought to take a look at him," Burt nodded in Fred's direction.

Fred gasped for air, then immediately closed his eyes and didn't move.

"What happened?" asked George.

"He probably couldn't handle the potion I gave him yesterday. Shame, I thought he was recovering well," the doctor shook his head.

Burt's eyes grew large and his jaw dropped. He felt the bottle in his pants pocket and froze at the sight of Fred.

George proceeded to unlock Burt's handcuff before escorting him out the building and back to Yuma Prison.

19: FIRE

Not only was it still cold when Burt got back to the prison but it had started to rain. Once he was left alone, he immediately tried to make himself throw up. Whatever was in that potion had killed old man Fred; and he did not want to become the next victim. Burt successfully vomited everything in his stomach into the thin layer of water now covering the floor of his cell from the relentless rain that dumped water for two hours. The whole prison was flooded along with all the cells. As the rain finally let up, Burt was allowed outside for his standard one hour. The sun was starting to set and the water was starting to drain away. His barf had even made a quick and convenient exit from his cell. With nothing better to do, Burt followed the flow of water as his fellow gang members watched from a distance. That was the first time Burt realized the prison was not level as he watched the water flow downward.

"He's gone crazy," said Bob.

"No, you two don't know him like I do. He's up to something," Billy studied Burt.

The water led to a narrow drain that went underground and popped up outside toward a normally dry creek. The dried up river however was not dry; instead, it had become a raging river. Burt thought the waterway most likely led to the Colorado River but he was not totally certain. Burt then rested his finger on his cheek and wondered how he could potentially use this drain and or the river to his advantage. Just then, he got it, he knew exactly what he wanted to do.

Over the next couple of weeks, Burt spent virtually every moment in his prison cell plotting their next great escape. The ideas in his head were so secretive that he didn't dare reveal anything to his gang for fear the information would leak out. He felt he could trust his men, but after Bill Downing backstabbed them, he knew he only had one true friend left in the world, and that was Billy Stiles. He and the men stayed away from George and Louis Owens who happily avoided them as well. He even got to thinking that Kate could turn on him. However, he had to try his luck and write Kate to send $20 to the doctor, which he did.

Weeks had passed. Knowing that if Kate had received his letter the money should have arrived for the doctor by now. Burt was restless and seriously considered faking an illness to go see the doctor. He was finally convinced that he should do it but before he could approach George, he summoned Burt to his office. Burt entered the office and watched George sift through some papers on his desk.

"Burt. Thanks for coming. Look, I want us to trust each other so I thought I'd give you some responsibility. You up for it?" asked George.

Burt coughed a few times before clearing his throat hoping the sound would alert George that he was falling ill, "Um, sure sir."

"Great. I hope you are not sick again by the sound of that cough. In any case this works out. The doctor who took care of you dropped off these potion bottles. I am putting you in charge of distributing it to the men who become ill. Take some for yourself since you're coughing, and keep them in your cell. After all, you took it and got better right away," said George.

Burt gave him a funny look, scratched his bald head and responded, "Happily."

"Great and because of your new responsibilities I will grant you the four-hour standard outside time. I hope this shows you that I am a forgiving man," said George.

"Yes sir, thank you," Burt said, and then exited smiling with the four potion bottles. Back in his cell, Burt wrapped the bottles inside a shirt and placed them underneath his bed. As he stood, he saw Billy outside his cell watching everything he was doing.

"Got something going on?" asked Billy.

Burt looked at him and then turned away saying only, "Fire."

"Just tell me the time and place. I can tell the men," said Billy.

"No. Don't tell them anything. Not certain I can trust them," said Burt.

"There as loyal as dogs," Billy argued.

"Perhaps, but I think it ought to be just you and me this time," he said. Burt then whispered his plan into Billy's ear. Billy's eyes opened wide as he listened to every detail. When Burt finished, Billy looked at Burt and had only one question, "So we are just going to have to wait then?"

"Yup. Could happen any day, just need another flood," Burt confirmed.

Weeks passed, then months, with hardly enough rain for Burt to execute his plan. Everything was prepped. It had become a waiting game which Burt got sick of. He hated being in prison. He hated the food, his cell, and everyone in the prison. He hadn't had a drink of alcohol in what seemed like forever. Though his dreams continued to haunt him at night, rest was not much of a problem because there was not much else to do. His dreams were now limited to escaping prison, dodging a bullet, and a Mr. Roosevelt talking to him over water with a woman by his side; he now believed that the water was a river. Burt lost his enthusiasm to read at the library and started to keep his distance from Bob, Bravo, and Chacon.

One night in mid-March 1901, however, was unlike any other. He was awoken by the sound of pellets on the ground outside. He sat up and listened as the noise grew stronger and stronger. This got his attention. He stood, put his hands on the bars and stared over toward Billy's cell to see if he was awake. He was, and he stood there as well seeing the rain and Burt.

A thin layer of water flooded the outside grounds and the cells. *More*, Burt thought to himself. After an hour Burt got his wish, the clouds opened up as the rain poured down. Burt signaled to Billy to tell him it was time. Just like Burt did in the last escape, he made sure the gate to his cell appeared to be locked but it wasn't. Billy's cell door had been manipulated as well. Burt checked his pockets to make sure he had the one item he needed before walking outside. Billy followed suit.

The rain continued to come down hard. Burt and Billy's running steps were easily disguised by the *tit-tat-tit-tat* of the rain. They ran toward George's office, first hiding next to the side of the building, the same place Burt and his gang had hidden once before. The water level on the ground was now higher; it did not seem to be draining away.

"Go Burt. Keep it dry," demanded Billy.

Burt checked his pocket again making sure he had what he needed. No light was coming from inside George's office so he stood from his crouch and ran. He stopped at the narrow drain that was supposed to be leading the water outside the prison. The drain sat slightly above ground level and was plugged by a rock. Burt pulled a box of matches from his pocket. He took out one match as the rain engulfed him. He tried to keep it dry but immediately realized that he would not be able to light it. He pulled out another one, more carefully this time covering it with his vest. However, rain leaked from his vest falling onto the match rendering it useless. Frustrated, he threw it on the ground grabbed another one.

Meanwhile, Billy was growing anxious. *What is taking so long*, he thought. But then Billy heard something from the opposite direction of Burt, and much closer. The door to George Bravin's office opened with a distinct creak. *Trouble*, Billy thought.

George walked outside holding his revolver. That was when Billy realized George had seen Burt. Billy did not know what to do. He thought about going back to his cell and jumping George at the same time. Instead, he just stood there watching.

Burt had successfully lit his fourth match attempt, pulled out the rock clogging the drain, and threw the match down the drain. Just as he threw it, Burt unsuspectingly heard, "Hands up," in George's familiar British accent. Burt turned around and looked at him.

"I thought we could trust each other, are you trying to escape again?" George looked disappointed.

"Look George, you shouldn't be here right now," said Burt.

"It's my job to be here," George replied as the rain slowly turned to a drizzle.

George grabbed Burt by his shirt collar and stood between him and the drain. Burt began slowly backing up as George aimed his revolver at Burt.

"I'm so sorry George, you don't deserve this," Burt said with a doleful look as he shielded his face with his arms and fell into the pond of water on the ground.

Just as George asked, "What?" the drain exploded. Burt felt the shock wave pass through him. Billy was able to turn his head away at the last second and covered his ears. Burt looked up and didn't see George anywhere, he was gone. Fire raged where the explosion occurred, but with it was also a wide escape hole. The flames quickly dissipated as the water had somewhere to go. Billy helped Burt up and led him by the shoulder to the hole. As they attempted to crawl their way out, they both slipped at the same time and were sucked down what was a river of mud and water downhill toward the old dry river. Thankfully, the river had filled with water and they were swept toward a cliff and dropped ten feet right into it. The river was like rapids and there was nothing to hold onto. Billy struggled to keep his head a float as Burt searched for any solution to get out.

Just ahead of them was a tree branch sticking out over the water. "This is our only chance, grab the tree branch!" Burt yelled to Billy. Billy, however, could not hear him, he was drowning. In a moment of hesitation, Burt had to decide whether to let his friend die or to save himself. *Ah hell,*

Burt thought. He heroically pulled Billy up and onto his shoulders just as they passed the tree branch. They continued on for another few minutes before the river dumped them into an even bigger river. However, this time the flow was not as fast.

"Hang on, Billy, we're in the Colorado River now," Burt called.

While it could not be determined by the sound of his voice Burt was getting tired. He again considered letting Billy drown and saving himself by using his body to keep him afloat. But before Burt could even make a decision, Billy spotted some wooden boards floating ahead.

"Look Burt," said Billy faintly.

Burt still held onto Billy as they caught up with the boards and grabbed onto the same one.

Billy laughed, "Just like you planned huh?"

The calmness of the river allowed them to steer to the river's edge. They crawled up onto the safety of the muddy ground where they laid soaked and out of breath. A few minutes passed before they spoke, Billy first, "Well that was fun. I doubted you there for a second but your plan always seems to come together. What now?"

Just as Burt began to respond it began to rain again. His sentences were short, "Back to Tombstone. Need to get Kate. We're done with the West."

20: THIRD CHANCE

The prison escape was the most newsworthy event the West had even witnessed. Not only did the outlaw Burt Alvord escape again, but he did so in the most unusual way; not to mention George Bravin had exploded in a hundred pieces. The remaining members of Burt's gang were intently questioned by Sheriff Frank Murphy on Burt's whereabouts and whether they had played any part in their escape. But none of the other three – Bob, Bravo, or Chacon – knew anything that would be helpful. Even brothers George and Louis Owens were questioned.

"Tell me Louis where Burt went and I can reduce your sentence," demanded Frank.

"I'm telling you I don't know nothing," said Louis.

"That's not good enough. Use your brain. Think," said Frank.

"I don't know … um I overheard a conversation Burt had with Billy not too long ago about a girl," Louis recalled.

"Girl?" asked Frank.

"I guess he's in love or something," said Louis.

"And the name?" asked Frank.

"Um … hmm … that's a good question. Can't remember. Something about a big nose," Louis replied.

"What did you say? Big nose?" questioned Frank.

"Yes, I think so," said Louis quizzically.

"There is only one person with that name in this region. I might just pay her a special visit," Frank said with a smirk.

Hundreds of miles away and two weeks after their escape, Burt and Billy made their way toward Tombstone. They stole horses, food, and clothing including hats from an unlucky family riding in a stagecoach that the men had come across.

It was late at night when they arrived in Tombstone. As they rode slowly into town so as not to draw any attention, they passed a Wanted Poster featuring their faces:

$15,000 Dollars, Dead or Alive

Upon seeing this, they pulled their hats down lower over their faces. They could not just simply walk into Kate's saloon being the most wanted men in the West. They would have to wait for the saloon to close for the night and meet Kate outside. Burt and Billy tied up their horses behind the saloon and sat down on the side of the building in the dark waiting.

"After you see her where are we going?" asked Billy.

"We've got to go somewhere away from this part of the United States. We could go south into Mexico but that would be obvious. We need to go north. Kate told me once she liked Colorado," said Burt.

Burt then stood as he heard Kate's voice in the near distance. Burt's head crept around the corner and he spotted Kate standing at the saloon entrance talking to a man. Burt and Billy could easily hear her conversation but neither of them knew the man she was talking to.

"They will be here soon I'm sure," Kate was saying.

"Well, it better be soon because I can't stay here much longer. People are going to start recognizing me," said the man.

"Are you sure you can provide them safety?" asked Kate.

"Have you forgotten who I am?" the man responded.

"Give it one more day at least," pleaded Kate.

"One more day, that's it," the man agreed.

Assuming she was talking about him and Billy, Burt left the shadows with Billy behind him.

"Looking for me?" Burt asked startling Kate and the man.

"Who's there?" the man demanded holding his hand on top of his gun resting in its holster.

"Alvord and Stiles," Burt called, his face was still cloaked by the darkness.

Kate, however, recognized his voice and ran over and hugged him tight. "I thought you died. The newspaper said no man could have survived that water," said Kate gleefully.

"You're the reason why I held on. I'll admit that I lost hope there for a bit though," Burt explained but was then interrupted by the man.

"I hate to break this up but we need to get a move on," said the man.

"And who are you?" asked Burt.

The man took a step backward so the streetlight could illuminate his face. He was an old man with a black mustache.

"I know who that is Burt. It's Wyatt Earp," Billy said in awe.

"At your service," said Wyatt.

Burt looked at the man in disbelief, it was really Wyatt Earp. After the famous gunfight, Wyatt had traveled all over the Western part of the United States doing various jobs in cities such as Seattle, San Francisco, San Diego, and most recently in the town of Nome, Alaska.

Burt thoughts immediately raced through his head of the gunfight that had killed his friend Frank McLaury. The thought of Frank reminded him that he no longer had his gun. Burt's thoughts turned to disgust as he looked at Wyatt Earp. "Why are you here?" Burt asked.

"One last favor for an old friend before my wife and I depart to Los Angeles where the both of you will be coming with," Wyatt explained.

Burt looked at Kate and asked, "What is happening?"

"You see, I knew somehow you would come back here. I called upon Wyatt to provide you with transportation to Los Angeles to escape this life," Kate said.

"I have a better idea, you and I leave for Colorado right now, you told me you liked it there," pleaded Burt.

"I liked it there when I visited Doc Holliday for the last time. I can't live there though; it would remind me of him too much. Besides, I can't just leave here, it would be too obvious and we'd both be in trouble. I need you to trust me, one day we will be together, stay patient," said Kate.

Burt looked down and sighed, "You're right." he said. Burt held her hand up and kissed it. Then he and Billy got onto their horses and followed Wyatt away into the night.

"Tomorrow morning, we stowaway on the train to Los Angeles, but tonight you two need to stowaway on the train somewhere where you won't be seen. I'd recommend the luggage car where the passengers' belongings are stored, no one will be in there when it leaves," said Wyatt.

"But people will still have luggage that will be placed inside the car from now until it leaves," said Billy.

"You're right, but I'm sure you two are smart enough to figure it out," said Wyatt.

Then Billy heard something that he'd never heard come out of Burt's mouth, "What's the plan?" Burt asked. Billy had always known Burt to be the one in charge, and it was odd to see Burt not in a position of leadership. Being that he asked this to the famous Wyatt Earp made it even crazier to, the man that had been a part of the gang who killed Frank McLaury and the other men.

"My wife and I will leave two horses tied up to the caboose car once we reach Los Angeles. We should be there at nighttime. You two need to make your way unseen, take those horses West, and stop at the farm of windmills. There will be hundreds of them. I will meet you two there. Don't mess this up, it is your second chance." said Wyatt.

"Third chance," Burt joked, "I've escaped prison twice."

Burt and Billy both agreed to the plan and left Wyatt as they headed to the train station. The train was in the station with no one around. They left their horses to roam free and then scoped out the luggage car. It was almost completely filled with trunks of clothing and belongings. Billy found a match and lit a lantern hanging in the middle of the ceiling. Burt and Billy were amazed at how full the car was and figured it would be worse the next day.

"We need to build some sort of fort with these trunks so we have enough room to sit and lay down," Billy suggested.

Burt did not answer. He'd started opening some of the trunks sifting through clothes, and household items.

"What are you doing?" asked Billy.

"Bound to be some money in one of these," Burt replied.

Billy joined Burt in his quest as they opened trunk after trunk not having any luck until eventually Billy discovered a trunk outlined with ornate gold trim. *This has to be the one*, Billy thought to himself. Instead, he opened it up to see something more valuable to Burt than money. "Burt, you need to see this."

Burt climbed over the other trunks and saw what Billy was looking at. His jaw dropped. "No!" announced Burt. It was his gun; the one that had once belonged to Frank McLaury and had last been in Sid the Kid's" possession. Burt held it up and examined it. "This is it, and it's still loaded," Burt said in astonishment.

"Well, if this gun's here that means that the Sid guy is on this train," Billy said.

"Probably on some sort of vacation using all the money he got. We better put a bullet between his eyes," said Burt.

"No Burt, if we do that, we will never be sent back to prison, we will be hung. Keep the gun if you must but I think you best leave it in his trunk. If he sees it is missing, he'll know you stole it," said Billy.

Burt, however, did not want to listen to Billy. "This isn't stealing if it already belonged to me. I'm keeping it," Burt stated defiantly. Burt then dug deeper into the trunk and pulled out a heavy bag. He opened it revealing a large sum of cash. "It must be the reward money," Burt laughed. "I sure would like to see the look on his face when he discovers that it's gone."

Billy did not respond, only shook his head at Burt while he looked at the cash.

21: WINDMILLS

Burt and Billy escaped with the gun and bag of cash as the train pulled into the Los Angeles train station. Two horses were waiting for them at the caboose just like Wyatt Earp said. It was the middle of the night, the air was cold, and they were not dressed for the weather. The wind numbed their noses, fingers, and toes as they rode west. Though it got cold in the desert from time to time they were taken back. They wished they'd also stolen some warm clothes from the trunks but had been unprepared for the chill. They were forced to stop after only a few minutes to search their saddlebags hoping that Wyatt had included something warm like blankets or even jackets. Each bag held the same items: a thin blanket, some bandannas, and one pair of socks.

"We'll have to deal with what we got. Cover your face with the bandanna, put the socks over your hands, and place the blanket inside your shirt," said Burt.

Billy and Burt fought through the next hour riding west until they finally reached the windmills. They rode up to the nearest one, jumped off their horses and waited for Wyatt. Burt rubbed the socks covering his hands together while Billy walked around in circles.

"What are you doing?" Burt asked.

"We need to keep moving or we will freeze," answered Billy.

Not long after Wyatt found them. As he got off his horse he laughed at the sight of them.

"Can't handle a little cold weather?" Wyatt grinned. He dug into his saddlebags and pulled out two thick wool jackets, which he threw to them. Burt and Billy put them on and immediately looked relieved. It felt like being snuggled by the sun.

Burt looked up hearing a swooshing noise as the windmill blades whipped through the air. He wondered if the sound had been there the whole time or if he just couldn't hear it before.

"Well done not being seen, we won't have problems for now," said Wyatt.

"Where too?" asked Billy.

"We'll meet my wife at our Los Angeles home. It's by the ocean, it will be some sight to see," said Wyatt.

Burt did not respond. When Wyatt mentioned the ocean, he immediately thought about his dreams, *Could this be it? The water he has seen so many times?* he asked himself.

"Burt, are you okay?" asked Wyatt.

Burt cleared his throat, "Yes, sorry let's go."

They climbed back onto their horses and made their way again westward. The sound of the windmill blades grew stronger as they passed under them.

Suddenly, Billy heard something and it did not like the windmills. "What's that noise?" asked Billy.

"That's just the windmills," Wyatt answered.

"No. Stop and listen," said Billy.

The three stopped and were silent as they tried to listen for what Billy heard.

Hoo, Hoo – there was an owl directly above them. Burt and Billy flinched but Wyatt stood his ground.

"There you go," Wyatt laughed but then he turned, he'd also heard something else.

"It's not the owl," said Billy.

"You're right, it's not," Wyatt agreed.

The sound was becoming louder and louder getting closer to the three men. Wyatt and Burt pulled out their guns while Billy just sat on his horse looking around; he had nothing to defend himself with.

"Where did you get a gun?" Wyatt asked Burt.

"This is actually mine, I found it in one of the trunks, it belongs to me," answered Burt.

"We have a problem then – it sounds like hoofbeats; I think someone is onto us," said Wyatt.

"Told you to leave the gun," Billy said to Burt frustrated.

"Relax, we have the famous Wyatt Earp on our side," said Burt.

The shadow of a horse could be seen in the near distance by the little moonlight the sky provided. Riding the horse was the outline of a man. He stopped in front of the men.

"State your business," demanded Wyatt.

"Not here for you Wyatt Earp," answered the man. "I'm here for my reward money, I could care less if you want the gun," the man glared at Burt.

"What is this man talking about," Wyatt asked Burt.

"That's Sid the Kid, the one responsible for taking my gun," Burt glared back at Sid.

"No, the reward money. Did you steal his money?" asked Wyatt.

"The way I see it; the money is mine as well," Burt argued.

Sid then hopped off his horse and Burt aimed his gun at him. Sid put his hands up indicating that he was unarmed. Wyatt and Billy observed the situation.

"Look here, *Outlaw* Burt, I'm done with you. I just want my money. You're clearly too smart to kept in prison. I'm moving to Los Angeles and won't be able to bother you anymore. I need that money to buy a house. You see I have big dreams," pleaded Sid.

"Give him the money!" yelled Wyatt.

"How do I know I can trust you?" Burt asked Sid.

"You can't I suppose. You'll just have to take my word for it. Stay out of my hair and I'll stay out of yours," said Sid.

Billy chuckled, "Burt got no hair."

Burt turned to Billy and frowned, then looked back at Sid. "Half the money," he suggested.

"No, I need it all," said Sid.

"Three-quarters then, final offer," Burt negotiated.

Sid shook his head and sighed, "Fine."

Burt grabbed a share from the bag and then threw it over to Sid. The Kid opened the bag and looked inside satisfied. "Good night boys," Sid climbed back onto his horse.

Burt filled with rage at the sight of the money bag in Sid's hand. He slowly pointed his gun at Sid's back as he rode off, placed his finger on the trigger, but then Billy stopped him. Billy lifted the gun up while Burt's hand was still holding it. Burt gave his friend a look of defeat and then accidentally shot a bullet into the air. The shock wave of the sound spooked Sid's horse and he kicked his legs back violently forcing Sid and the bag of cash to fall. The horse ran off into the night.

"Ah heck," Wyatt spat and then rode to Sid's aid. Sid was not moving laying on his back. Wyatt jumped off his horse and knelt down to examine Sid. Wyatt felt his chest to see if it was moving but it wasn't. He snapped his fingers in front of Sid's eyes and gave him a light slap on the face. Wyatt then felt the back of Sid's head and noticed it was wet. He sniffed the liquid and realized right away it was blood. He whipped the blood on the ground and took a long deep breath before joining Burt and Billy.

"He's dead. Back of head smashed onto a rock," said Wyatt.

"What did I do?" Burt asked himself out loud in confusion. He then went to see for himself. He got of his horse and dropped to his knees next to Sid's body. His mind felt cluttered with regret. He was suddenly questioning everything he had ever done.

"It's over Burt," said Wyatt.

Burt continued to remain on his knees as a single tear rolled down the side of his face. He saw a younger version of himself in Sid filled with hope and promise, and now he'd destroyed his future. Billy saw the bag of cash next to Sid's body and held it up for Burt to see.

"I guess this here is yours now Burt," Billy called.

Burt shook his head. "No, it stays with him. We'll bury him with it here underneath this windmill," muttered Burt.

Billy had heard the tone in Burt's voice change; it was something he hadn't heard since they were kids.

"Okay Burt, the money stays with him," Billy agreed.

The three dragged Sid's body to the next nearest windmill and buried his body. Once done, Burt stood over the grave, put his hands on his hips and told himself, *I've got to change*.

22: LOS ANGELES

L os Angeles provided a much different lifestyle than Burt and Billy were accustomed to. Wyatt and his wife occupied a home near the ocean while he put Burt and Billy up in an apartment building in downtown Los Angeles on Broadway Street. After having done this as a favor to Kate, Wyatt did not plan on seeing them ever again.

Burt thought the Pacific Ocean was going to be what he had dreamed of but he was wrong. Never once did he see the water. He was too busy where he was. It was a bustling city with everyone always on the move. The roads were shared by horse-drawn wagons, bicycles, pedestrians, and electric trolley cars which chugged on tracks down the middle of the road. While Burt enjoyed the energy of the new location, Billy was amazed at modern advancements. Electricity lit up the city at night, illuminating building signs, and the power of one light bulb rather than numerous candles lit up the inside of people's homes. There was an electric lamp in their apartment, which fascinated Billy. He was amazed that all they had to do was turn a switch to turn it on and off. Rather than getting their water from a well, it was easily assessable from their sink.

* * *

A year had passed and it was now November 1903. While word of their great prison escape had been the local newspaper from time to time followed by occasional wanted and reward signs, it was largely quiet. No one seemed to recognize them. Billy had grown a patchy beard while Burt sported a thick short one. Wyatt found them both jobs at the Los Angeles Sanitation Department cleaning up horse manure from the city streets. The work was not luxurious but their faces were rarely seen since they wore hats and kept their heads down. Nevertheless, it paid the apartment rent.

Burt constantly thought of Kate, wondering when the day would come and they'd be with one another. He wrote her letters monthly using Wyatt's name as the return address for fear of being caught. One day after finishing one of those letters, Burt left the apartment to drop it off at the post office before going to work. He successfully mailed it, but as he walked out of the building, he stopped seeing a commotion across the street at the bank. He saw a woman screaming as she ran out of the bank, "Robbery!"

People around her ran the other way. Gunshots could be heard – *bang, bang, bang* – from inside the bank. Burt started walking in the opposite direction but something made him stop. He was suddenly over-whelmed with an idea to help but came to the conclusion that he would be risking his new opportunity. Sid's death had affected him, and he wanted to be a changed man. While he was tempted occasionally by a drink of alcohol, he had been able to shy away from it. The long duration he'd been without alcohol during his last prison sentence seemed to have sobered him up.

Three robbers then ran out of the bank holding heavy bags while firing their guns in the air. People took off in all directions in a panic. Burt understood what the men were doing. They wanted to clear a path to escape, yet not leave any blood on their hands. Burt's former lawman instincts seemed to kick in and he could not stand the sight of the three men escaping. *Ah hell*, he thought to himself. Burt then spotted a trolley car full of people heading toward the scene and didn't appear to be stopping. The electric cables above the trolley sparked giving Burt an idea. He ran as fast as he could and jumped onto the trolley, he climbed up onto its roof just as the robbers, now on their horses, were riding quickly in their direction. Two antennas were connected from the roof to the cable lines. People in the surrounding area now stood in amazement and confusion to what was happening. Burt got ahold of the antennas and in a sheer moment of strength he snapped the cable line forcing the trolley to come to an immediate halt, as the cable lines to fell to the ground still sparking with electricity. The cables whipped unpredictably across the ground scaring the robber's horses. The three men tried desperately to hang on but were all forced to jump. Now left with no plan, the outlaws looked around aimlessly for a horse to steal but were unable to act now that they were surrounded by cable lines. Even though the whole event only lasted about sixty seconds it was enough time for policemen on horseback to reach the scene.

People applauded Burt for his heroic act and Burt quickly put his head down. *What did I just do?*" he thought. He quickly climbed down from the trolley roof and ran. As he did, he saw a familiar face, only the man was now much older, but Burt could not stop, he had to get away. He entered the apartment building slamming the door and out of breath.

"You were supposed to meet me on Second Street, not back here. Why are you out of breath?" asked Billy.

"Messed … up … bad," Burt tried to catch his breath.

"What did you do now?" Billy questioned with a serious look.

"Stopped a robbery, a lot of people saw me," answered Burt.

"You did what?" demanded Billy.

Burt peeked out the window to see if anyone had followed. He scanned left and right down the street a few times, but everything looked normal.

"How many people saw you?" asked Billy.

"I don't know, a dozen or so," said Burt.

"Well, I sure as hell hope no one recognizes you at work today," Billy said.

Burt's face looked grim, "There's another problem. I recognized someone and they saw me. I might be going crazy but I'm pretty sure it was George Parsons, the man who owned the library in Tombstone. He was good friends with Wyatt Earp, if he realizes it was me then he will surely tell him."

Billy started to get upset, and sternly began telling Burt what do, something he rarely did. "If you don't show your face then there won't be a problem. Just go about your business like normal and keep your head down. Besides, I'm not doing that disgusting job alone."

Burt sighed, but agreed with Billy. They left their apartment and went to start their long grueling shift. When they reached the street they were tasked to clean that day, they stopped, shocked by how bad it was. Piles and piles of horse manure littered the road. Flies swarmed and a bicyclist drove over it, but the worst part was that most of the manure had dried up, which meant that when the wind blew it would dust the sidewalks where people were walking. There wasn't a cloud was in the sky but the heat was bearable. Burt and Billy started filling their hand-pulled carts with manure. Their only weapons against the manure consisted of brooms and shovels.

They got to work as Billy scoffed at every shovelful he threw into his wagon. *I need to get out of this place*, Billy thought to himself.

Burt was only worried about being recognized or seeing George again. He covered his face with a bandanna which not only provided protection from being noticed, but also slightly shielded the manure stench. Burt heard chattering among the surrounding people, saying things like: *Did you hear what happened*? and *He's a hero*. Burt knew they were talking about the incident. He kept his face down and continued to shovel manure with Billy for the rest of the day until the sun went down.

The next morning, Billy left to get the day's newspaper despite his aching body from the previous day. Burt had urged him to go and get it as he figured news about the bank robbery would be featured.

Billy arrived back at the apartment and tossed the paper on the kitchen table, the headline read: *Trolley Car Man Saves the Day*

The story described Burt's heroism and how he should make an appearance at court while the robbers were sentenced to prison in a future day to be acknowledged. The story did not describe Burt's appearance except that people said he had been well built and strong as an ox. While Burt read, he was relieved but at the same time concerned that someone was still out there who might recognize him. Then, the last sentence put fear in Burt's head. If the men were sent to prison, it could be to Yuma Prison.

"If those men can accurately describe me to Bob, Bravo, Chacon, or even the Owens' brothers our cover will be blown," Burt said to Billy.

Just then, there was an unexpected knock at their apartment door. Burt stayed back as Billy walked over to it. Billy grasped the handle but called out first, "Who is it?"

"Wyatt," the man stated.

Billy opened the door and Wyatt stormed in followed by another man. Wyatt was holding the newspaper. Burt immediately recognized the man behind Wyatt, it was George Parsons. "Do you have rocks for brains?" Wyatt yelled tossing the newspaper at his chest. He then sat in a chair in the middle of the room. "Now we have to come up with a new plan."

23: THE PLAN

Wyatt figured with the inevitability of the robbers going to Yuma Prison that they had a few weeks to get ahead of anyone that might come after Burt and Billy. Wyatt felt obligated to help the two because he was now tied into all this. They agreed to take the day to think about where they should go. While Wyatt was willing to help them, he'd decided that he could no longer live in the same town or city as Burt or Billy.

"After we come up with the plan, you two are on your own," said Wyatt.

George spoke next, "Sorry Burt, I had to tell Wyatt."

Wyatt and George then left the apartment saying they'd return later that night after giving a plan some thought. Burt paced around the apartment for most of the day thinking hard. He was not afraid to go to a new town but Billy was. Billy missed the heat of the desert and the place where he grew up. Despite the luxury of having running water and electricity, Billy was still homesick. Burt gave up on thinking and grabbed the newspaper once again. He sat on his bed and began reading the advertisements and stories. He read the article again about his heroism. He shook his head as he thought: *I could have been the best lawman.* Businesses advertised food, clothing, shoes, and furniture. He then came across an interesting article on the Panama Canal. The United States was taking control of the

French-owned property and soon workers would be needed. The job even provided three meals daily, and lodging to anyone hired.

"Perhaps that's it!" Burt announced.

"Huh?" asked Billy.

Burt's enthusiasm continued, "If we stay in the United States or Mexico we'll surely get caught. We need to go somewhere where we can work and where no one will know us; like the Panama Canal."

"What? No, no I don't plan on leaving this country. I plan on going right back where I came from," said Billy.

"You can't do that. Have you forgotten you're still a fugitive, a man on the run? They will hang you if you're caught," Burt advised.

"I just want to live my life. I don't want to be a man on the run Burt," said Billy. Billy then turned away, afraid to say the next thing, but found the courage to speak his mind, "We will have to go our separate ways one day soon."

Burt nodded slowly as he said, "You're right, I agree."

Billy raised his head and fixed his eyes on Burt. "Well, it sounds like one last adventure. What's the plan?" asked Billy.

Burt stood in the middle of the room while Billy leaned against the wall. Burt looked at the newspaper not knowing exactly what to say. His eyes briefly scanned over the word *cash*, which triggered his brain to remember all the cash stashed under the farmhouse in Mexico. His thoughts then turned to Kate. Billy watched Burt knowing that was processing the information. He stayed patient until Burt said, "I got it!"

Burt waited until Wyatt and George returned that night to tell Billy and the other two about his plan.

"Alright this is what I came up with. Billy and I are going to take the same route back to Tombstone," Burt explained and Wyatt's eyes lit up looking at him as if he was crazy. "We'll have to ride back through the windmills at night and hide in the luggage train car again. Wyatt, we'll need you to provide horses for us once the train stops. After that, Wyatt, we won't see you ever again. Billy plans to stay in Tombstone while Kate and I will leave together to pick up the cash I left in Mexico, then we'll head south to the Panama Canal."

Wyatt frowned as he thought about the probability of it working. "While it's much different than what I was thinking, you could pull this off. However, I won't be going with you two to Tombstone. You'll need to find someone else to get the horses. I also think that you'll have a hard time convincing Kate to join you." Wyatt then turned to Billy, "Why would you stay in Tombstone?"

"I need to go home," responded Billy.

George then walked over to Billy, "Look man, I can't tell you what to do but what I will say is that you have an opportunity to keep living. If you go back there, you'll be hung and buried with the others in Boothill Graveyard."

At the mentioning of Boothill, both Burt and Billy immediately thought of the famous gunfight. Boothill was where the men who died by the hands of Wyatt, Morgan, Virgil, and Doc Holliday, including Burt's friend Frank McLaury had been laid to rest.

Billy said nothing as he was still not convinced.

"My wife and I discussed this and we've decided to stay here. We have a successful saloon we just opened, and she loves the ocean. I'm offering you a job Billy if you want it. Plenty of money, women, and booze," Wyatt grinned.

"Do it Billy. Stay in Los Angeles with Wyatt. I can do this alone. I can't stand the idea of you being caught and hung. Please Billy, do it," pleaded Burt.

Billy took a long deep breath before answering, "Fine – one last favor for my longtime friend. Just like you Wyatt did for Kate."

"It's settled then other that the horse," George said. "When is the next train to Tombstone?"

Burt picked up the newspaper and said, "Tomorrow – once I figure out a horse for myself, and if not, I will walk it."

Billy looked at Burt with sadness. This would be the last time he'd see his friend. Burt would either be caught, killed, or living a new life and die an old man. Wyatt and George shook Burt's hand and wished him good luck. Wyatt told Billy he'd talk to him soon and then he left the apartment with George.

Billy then walked over to the shelf that housed their food. He shuffled around some cans before pulling out a whiskey bottle. He showed it to Burt and asked, "One last drink?"

Burt smiled and nodded. Billy poured two glasses and handed one to Burt. That night they shared stories of their youth, in particular about the owner of the O.K. Corral, *Honest John* Montgomery. They joked about how he hated when they were late and how he was always so organized keeping meticulous notes in his notebook.

"Whatever happened to him and his notebook?" asked Burt.

"Oh, he got shot by a cowboy who thought he had been wronged. I don't know about the notebook. Still to this day, I don't know why he took so many notes," said Billy.

"I know why, he showed me once. It was his business journal. He recorded every rental. He never wanted to run the O.K. Corral, instead he dreamed of one day being a baseball player with the Chicago Cubs. Apparently, he was a good baseball player once," said Burt.

"Have you thought about what you're going to say to Kate?" asked Billy.

"Not much other than telling her if she loves me, she'll go with me," said Burt.

"Wyatt for some reason showed little confidence in that, do you know why?" asked Billy.

"I think Wyatt still considers Kate as Doc Holliday's girl even though he's dead. In any case I'm going to try my best to convince her," said Burt.

Later that night Burt and Billy went to bed. It was quiet in the apartment other than the faucet leaking an occasional drip of water. The silence was soon broken by Burt shuffling in his bed. Billy opened one eye to see his friend struggling like he did most nights. Familiar with his friend's nighttime behavior Billy closed his eye and tried to go back to sleep. However, minutes later Burt was breathing heavily and rapidly sat up screaming, "No!" multiple times.

"Burt. Wake up, you're dreaming again!" Billy yelled as he stood and walked over to Burt. But just as he reached the foot of the bed Burt fell back into his pillow and immediately started snoring. Billy saw the expression on Burt's face; he was smiling which Billy figured meant that Burt's dreams were over for the night. Billy got back into his bed but could not sleep for the rest of the night, he felt sad that he'd never see his friend again after tomorrow. While it was a long night for Billy, Burt woke up refreshed.

"I had the weirdest dream last night," said Burt.

"Different from the usual?" asked Billy.

"Yes. You were in it this time. You were a hero," said Burt.

Burt got up and dressed, ate a large breakfast and stocked his bag with canned goods. He fixed his hat on his large bald head before grabbing his beloved gun.

"I want you to have this to remember me by. I can get a new one. Besides, you're a better shot than I am," said Burt.

He handed the gun to Billy who seemed confused at first but then accepted the gift. They shook each other's hands, stared at one another with a look of sadness, then Burt let go, walked out the door, and he was gone.

24: HOSTAGE

Burt rode his horse the same route to the train station that he and Billy had taken when they'd arrived in Los Angeles. His mind was focused, he knew what his task was, and to him nothing would stand in his way. He came upon the windmills which were turning slowly with the little flow of wind in the air. He stopped at Sid's grave. Burt climbed off his horse, and talked to Sid for a moment. He apologized and vowed to live the rest of his life justly. Knowing that he most likely would never be there again he tossed some dirt on top of Sid's grave to honor him. Burt then got up, tipped his hat, climbed back onto his horse and pushed on. He was about a mile away when he saw the train in the distance. A light plume of smoke rose from its smokestack indicating it would not be long before it was ready to leave. It was still light and Burt would not have the luxury of darkness to hide on the train. He kicked his horse with his heels and forced it to sprint; however, as the horse took off, Burt realized it was kicking up a lot of dirt. He did not want to draw attention so he had no choice but to stop the horse, grab his supplies, and continue on foot. He threw his sack over his shoulder and ran as fast as his boots would take him. The train whistle screamed loudly, and slowly inched forward. Burt was only a quarter of a mile out but he couldn't stop. Some passengers began to notice him from the windows; some even cheered him on as the train gained momentum.

"You can do it!" yelled a passenger.

He was ten feet away from the train but it was getting away. Burt pushed forward, though heavily out of breath. His side began hurting and his feet throbbed. Five feet from the train, only three cars were left. Just as he was a foot away, he grabbed the metal bar of the caboose and barely made it on. He hoisted his body up toward the door and lay down out of breath. Within moments he felt sick. Burt leaned to his side and threw up his breakfast. As he slowly caught his breath, the door kicked open and hit Burt in the leg. A man stood over him with a smile.

"That was a gallant effort, please come in," the man reached out his hand.

Burt did not know if he should, but could see that the man did not recognize him. He grasped his hand and the man pulled him up. The man patted him on the back and asked him to follow him to his cabin. The man was wearing an expensive black suit with a gold pocket watch attached to his jacket. As they passed a few other passengers, Burt put his head down, but thankfully they were almost immediately inside the man's cabin.

"Sit down, please," said the man.

"Thank you," said Burt.

"Hungry?" asked the man.

"Thirsty," replied Burt.

The man turned and poured Burt a glass of water into an ornate glass cup. It was clear that the man was wealthy by the way he dressed and spoke. He handed Burt the glass of water and said, "I am H.M. Dubois," in a French accent.

Burt appreciated his kind gesture but didn't want to stay long. He finished his water and told Mr. Dubois he needed to leave. However, Mr. Dubois insisted he stay wanting the conversation rather than traveling in silence on his trip to Tombstone. Burt agreed though he was reluctant to talk with the man. Burt considered telling him his real name but knew it was best to lie.

"I am Matt Burts," said Burt.

"Nice to meet you Mr. Burts, what brings you to this fine train on this fine day?" Mr. Dubois asked.

"Visiting an old friend in Tombstone, she is sick," said Burt.

"So sorry to hear that, no wonder you ran so hard. I am visiting on business. I own a number of buildings in the western half of the United States and have a potential tenant that wants to take over an old saloon," said Mr. Dubois.

"Sounds like you've made a good living for yourself," said Burt.

"Yes, and what do you do Mr. Burts?" asked Mr. Dubois.

"Mostly in the mining business myself," Burt responded.

"Ah, mining. Filthy business, no?" asked Mr. Dubois.

"Yes, but there's money to be made," said Burt.

"*Ha*, good man – how about a drink?" Mr. Dubois offered.

"None for me thanks," said Burt.

Mr. Dubois insisted though, ignoring Burt's response. He pulled out two more glasses and poured each of them some red wine. Burt pretended to sip the wine; he'd never had an affinity for it. Mr. Dubois though drank it quickly and got up several times to refill his glass. By his fifth glass, Mr. Dubois was drunk and did not notice that Burt was still on his first glass.

"What saloon in Tombstone are you talking about Mr. Dubois?" asked Burt.

"Oh, I believe it's been called Big Nose Kate's Saloon for some time. She doesn't want to run it anymore, apparently she's working a farm now, so I'm meeting someone I know who is interested in running the saloon," said Mr. Dubois.

Burt could not hide his expression – his eyes lit up and his palms began to sweat. *Oh no, how will I find her?* he thought.

Mr. Dubois slurred some words, then got up and landed face first passing out drunk in his bed. Just as he hit the bed, the train started slowing, eventually coming to a stop. "*It's too early for us to be here,*" Burt looked out the window and saw nothing but desert and a few buildings off in the distance. He focused on the buildings and realized that they were near Yuma. Just then, Burt heard gunfire followed by a door slamming open outside the cabin. Burt slowly opened the cabin door and peeked out. A long-bearded man was holding a gun up, his face fully covered with a bandanna except his eyes. Upon seeing this, Burt immediately shut the door which drew the man's attention. The man stood outside the cabin door and kicked it open.

"Hands up. All your valuables in the bag!" yelled the man.

Mr. Dubois continued to sleep while Burt threw his hands in the air.

"Burt? Is that really you?" asked the man.

He then uncovered his face revealing his identity. It was Chacon.

Burt was shocked and struggled for words before finally asking, "What in the hell are you doing here?"

"We just escaped from prison, boy will Bob and Bravo love to see this. They're holding up the conductor. We need some money before we can hide out in the mountains," said Chacon.

Burt then turned to Mr. Dubois and fished inside the sleeping man's pocket finding his wallet. He pulled out his watch as well and threw both items in his bag.

"Take this and go. I'm heading back to Tombstone to get Kate and leave this here country," said Burt.

"On no. You don't call the shots anymore. You left us to rot in that prison. The way I see it, you're more valuable than any piece of jewelry I'll find here. We're going to turn you in," Chacon said.

"What? How can you do that? You guys are all fugitives," Burt argued.

"We'll figure it out," said Chacon who then pointed his gun at Burt. "Get up!" he demanded.

Burt looked at him sternly but stood with his hands up. Chacon escorted him outside toward the caboose and then to the ground where Chacon's horse waited. Chacon jumped onto his horse and continued to point his gun at Burt. "Start walking toward the front of the train or I'll shoot," Chacon ordered.

Chacon paraded Burt alongside the train cars for all the passengers to see. Burt looked into the windows at the passengers who looked frightened by what they were witnessing. Burt though only hoped that no one recognized him. Just as they reached the front of the train, Bob and Bravo poked their heads out of the conductor's room.

"Oh, bloody hell," said Bravo.

"No way," said Bob.

"Yes boys, it seems that we have a hostage on our hands now," said Chacon.

Bravo punched Burt in the gut. "That's for leaving us," said Bravo.

"Let's tie him up," Bob threw a long rope to Chacon.

Chacon got off his horse and tied Burt's wrists. He then made Burt jump up onto his own horse while Chacon jumped on behind Burt.

"Yeehaw!" yelled Bravo as they sped away from the train with their new hostage.

25: A FAMILIAR PLACE

They made their way to the mountains far from civilization where they planned to camp out for the time being. Burt felt like a defeated man. He did not fight the situation, only accepting it as his fate. He had wronged these men, so he believed he had it coming. He had no idea when or if he'd have an opportunity to escape from his old gang but he did have one advantage, he knew each of the men's personalities. Though Chacon had painted himself as the new leader, he could be easily swayed. Bravo and Bob, who were the most loyal men besides Billy, were not the leadership type. Burt knew his best chance of survival was to convince the men that they needed him.

The men set up camp deep in the mountains and tied Burt to a large boulder where he was only able to sit and not lay down comfortably. Burt had no weapons or belongings except the clothes on his back. The men sat around the campfire and discussed what they should do with Burt while he listened.

"Why don't we just shoot him here? He will be nothing but trouble," said Bob.

"No. We need him to get the reward money," said Chacon.

"And who declared you leader?" Bravo asked Chacon.

"I'm the one that got us out of that prison, so I declare myself leader," said Chacon.

"That sure was funny. Who would have thought the keys to the front gate would have accidentally been left inside the keyhole? Too easy," Bob laughed.

"Okay since long beard over there has decided he's the leader, what do you propose as your plan for bringing him in? We can't do it," said Bravo.

Chacon mumbled something but before he could say anything clearly Burt intervened.

"You'll have to take me to someone who lives on the outskirts of town and convince them to take me in. It shouldn't be hard if you offer them a cut of the money," said Burt.

"Why would you help us?" asked Bravo.

"I wronged all of you. Fate allowed you to capture me. I might as well make you rich," Burt explained.

"He's lying, he's always up to something," Bob announced.

"Quiet! let the man speak. I like your plan Burt, we will take you to Yuma first thing in the morning," said Chacon.

"What? We just escaped from that town. Why would we go back there?" Bravo questioned.

"No, not to Yuma. I happen to know that the reward is higher if you take me to Tombstone – somewhere around $25,000 alive." Burt's demeanor remained calm; he knew all too well that their eyes would light up at that number. They were still on a high having just recently escaped from prison and now finding gold in Burt's capture.

"You hear that boys? We're going to be rich," Chacon said confidently.

"Sounds pretty risky to me but I'm in," said Bob.

Bravo was not ready to accept the plan. "What's your angle here Alvord?" Bravo looked over at Burt.

"No angle," Burt answered, "I'm telling you the truth. My life as an outlaw is over."

"They'll hang you though," said Bravo.

"Not without a fair trial. I'll receive a longer prison sentence this time," said Burt.

Bravo nodded slowly and looked at Chacon and Bob saying, "Fine, I'm in."

That night, they left Burt tied to the boulder. He barely got any sleep while the three men slept soundly on the ground next to the campfire. By the start of sunrise, the fire had burned out and it remained mostly quiet. Burt was first to hear the sound and his head popped up. Several rattlesnakes slithered around in the dirt next to the men. Burt wasn't sure if waking them was best or whether to just let the snakes pass by. He thought the possibility of startling the men would cause the snakes to react so he stayed quiet.

One of the snakes crawled over the top of Chacon's boot, followed by another that brushed Bob's hand. Chacon woke up first immediately seeing the snake, screamed, "*Ahh.*"

The snakes' rattles began to shake violently in response. They looked prepared to strike. The noise alarmed Bravo and Bob who quickly awoke and jumped to their feet.

"No any sudden movements," Bravo whispered.

Chacon though stepped backward and tripped over a log, and let out another scream. The snakes all pounced then, one's fangs sank into Bob's forearm, another struck Bravo in the thigh, and yet another got Chacon in the neck. The men belted out terrifying yells immediately in pain.

Burt could only watch in horror. Chacon was on the ground not moving while Bravo and Bob ran in opposite directions to get away. The snakes were not far from Burt now.

"Untie me!" Burt pleaded.

However, Bravo and Bob were too worried about their wounds and ignored Burt's plea. A few of the snakes rolled over Chacon and were getting even closer.

"Help!" demanded Burt.

Suddenly, gunshots started raining over the campsite. The bullets hit two of the snakes then struck Bravo and Bob. Both men instantly fell to the ground and weren't moving. Burt believed them to be dead but couldn't check. Burt then heard footsteps. They got louder and louder and a man dressed in all black matching his black mustache arrived on the scene. The man held two guns which were still smoking. As the man turned toward Burt, he knew exactly who it was, Jeff Milton.

"Well, I'll be damned. I came out here on a regular old manhunt and find you. You got a lot of guts staying in the area," Jeff said.

"You're quiet the tracker. Care to help an old friend and untie me?" Burt asked calmly.

"Friend – I'll show you what kind of friend I am. We're going straight back to Willcox so I can show you off to all the townspeople, the ones who once looked up to you. They'll take great pleasure in seeing you hang," said Jeff. He then checked to see if there was any life left in Chacon, Bravo, and Bob, but all three were dead.

Jeff left Burt tied up as he threw the dead men one by one over his shoulder placing two bodies on one horse to take them back to Willcox and provide proof of their deaths and Jeff's heroics. Burt noticed that Jeff winced every time he lifted one of the bodies. It was clear that his shoulder was not the same after being shot, but nevertheless; Burt was surprised by how strong he actually was. Jeff then untied Burt from the boulder but rewrapped his hands into a tight knot. He then escorted Burt to the only vacant horse which was Chacon's, helped him on it, then grabbed the reins of the three horses and pulled Burt and the dead men behind him back to Willcox.

A few days later they made it into town. Jeff paraded the dead bodies as well as Burt down the same road where Burt had once been humiliated. The townspeople stared at the dead bodies in horror and were shocked at seeing Burt. The line of horses continued as seemingly everyone in town watched until Jeff stopped at Burt's old jailhouse. Jeff tied the horse Burt was riding to the post outside the building, while a hundred or so people watched as Jeff threw Burt inside the jailhouse. They applauded and cheered for Jeff who happily soaked up the moment. A few folks even threw eggs at Burt as he was paraded through town.

Jeff stood on the steps outside the Sheriff building and addressed the crowd, "I have defeated the great outlaw, Burt Alvord. Never again will he reign his terror in this town or the West. Tomorrow, I propose we skip trial and hang him. Who agrees with me?"

Everyone yelled in agreement and raised their fists in the air.

"*How am I going to get out of this*," Burt thought. Just then a younger man wearing a Silver Star joined Jeff.

"He's all yours for the night Sheriff. I leave it up to you to keep an eye on him," said Jeff.

"Eyes will be on him all night," said the Sheriff.

The crowd, including Jeff left the scene and it was just the Sheriff and Burt.

The Sheriff held a rifle as he spoke with Burt. "Best not try any funny business, we know how you escaped before," said the Sheriff.

"What's your name kid?" asked Burt.

"You can call me Sheriff Tom," the man answered.

Burt did not like the idea of such a young kid being in charge of his old post. Rather than picking an argument, Burt decided that he needed to spend every moment he had to think about escaping. The Sheriff left and went to his office, which gave Burt a moment to sit down and reflect. It was warm in the jailhouse, barely any air flowed in from the outside. Based on the Sheriff's words, Burt figured escape through the tunnel was out of the question, though it would not stop him from taking a peek when the sun went down. He sat in the chair with his thoughts as he waited for darkness staring at the wooden boards that made up the walls in the very familiar place.

26: THE SHOT

It was now nightfall and Burt looked out the window to see if the Sheriff was around. As he did, the door to the office opened and the Sheriff walked over holding a half-eaten chicken wing and a cup of whiskey. *Bang, Bang, Bang* – the Sheriff knocked on the door loudly, stuck the key in the keyhole and opened the door. "Last meal," said Sherriff Tom who threw Burt the chicken wing and set the cup down. Burt could smell the whiskey radiating from his breath. The Sherriff then slammed the door and walked back into the office.

Burt immediately lifted the square-shaped wooden board up from the floor which led down the tunnel to the office. He climbed down and started crawling. Almost instantly Burt knew something was wrong. The path was blocked; the tunnel must have caved in at some point. Burt had to crawl backward to return to where he'd started. Once back inside, he slammed his fist on the floor and said, "What now?"

Clink – there was a noise to his right. Something had fallen. Burt investigated by feeling the floor with his bare hands. His left hand touched something sharp and thin. Burt pulled his hand back thinking he he'd just been bitten by something. Nothing moved in response so he reached down again, this time picking it up. It was the nail object with the hook-shaped end, and the initials 3FJ inscribed on the flat side. *Three Fingered Jack*! *Aha*! Burt said to himself. It was the same nail he'd stuck underneath the chair back when he, Bob, and Billy had escaped before. Burt's heart raced fast. For the first time in forever he felt nervous. He had a chance to escape, but he had to do it at the right time. He feared Jeff Milton was waiting outside hidden, and thought Sheriff Tom would come outside any minute. Burt took a deep breath and decided, *I need to be patient.*

He sat down next to the half-eaten chicken wing and cup of whiskey waiting for it to get later in the night. He was neither hungry nor thirsty. A couple of hours passed before Burt stood again and looked out the window. The coast was clear but he heard the sound of hammering nails into wood in the distance. "I bet they are building the gallows where I'll be hung," said Burt. As the sound of each nail was pounded Burt felt like he was hearing the music to his funeral. He now had a sense of urgency to get out. He reached out the open window with his left arm his hand holding the nail and found the keyhole. He heard Bob's voice in his head saying, *Place the end of the nail at an angle and then, slowly twist until you hear a click.*

Click, the door opened. Burt threw the nail into some nearby bushes and ran toward the horse still tied up in front of the office. As Burt got to his horse, he could hear the Sheriff drunkenly singing from inside the office. Burt shook his head, untied and mounted the horse and slowly and quietly guided the horse away so as not to draw attention. As soon as he turned the corner he took off. Though he was a few blocks away Burt spotted a handful of men building the gallows. As soon as he was a few hundred feet outside the town Burt slowed the horse to a walking pace figuring he was in the clear. Burt took a deep breath and glanced at the stars. It was a calm night with little wind.

"He escaped!" a voice yelled from inside town.

Burt could hear this clearly. Before he could take off again, he had to decide which direction to go: Tombstone, the farmhouse, or head toward Panama. He rested his hand behind him for a moment and felt Chacon's saddlebag. Burt grabbed it and looked inside hoping there would be a weapon. However, to his surprise there was no weapon at all, only a wallet and the gold pocket watch that Chacon had stolen from Mr. Dubois.

Think, just think? Burt thought.

Burt took a deep breath and looked up at the stars again this time seeing a shooting star heading in the direction of Tombstone. "Fate?" Burt questioned. "Guess I best return Mr. Dubois's belongings; I'll probably find him at Kate's saloon." Burt forced his horse onward, sprinting much of the night as it turned into morning. He didn't give the horse a break and reached Tombstone in record time.

It was the afternoon of the next day when he arrived. He didn't want to draw attention to himself so he searched with the saddlebag for something to cover his face. Luckily, the saddlebag contained a bandanna, which Burt used to cover his face only revealing only his bald head. The sun was warm and Burt's head began to turn red. He tied up the horse at a nearby hotel, and confidently walked at a normal pace as if he was just going about his everyday business. Shortly he reached his destination, he made it into Kate's saloon unnoticed.

Inside the saloon, Mr. Dubois and another man stood next to the bar. Burt revealed his face to them and Mr. Dubois responded by telling the man to politely step away to talk to Burt.

"Are you here to rob me again?" Mr. Dubois asked with hands on his hips.

Burt reached into the bag and Mr. Dubois quickly stepped backward holding his hands up. "What do you want from me?" he questioned.

Burt pulled out his wallet and gold pocket watch. "I came to return these. I wasn't the one who stole them, but I got them back from the person who did," Burt explained.

Mr. Dubois smiled and took back his belongings.

Suddenly the saloon doors slammed open. "Hands up!" screamed a man.

Burt sighed at the sight of the man; it was Jeff Milton again; he'd tracked him down. "You never give up do you?" asked Burt.

"Enough with these games, enough with you, I am going to end this now," Jeff pointed his gun at Burt.

Mr. Dubois backed away and hid behind a pool table.

"Just hold on a moment," pleaded Burt as he inched toward to the pool tables as well.

"Enough!" yelled Jeff. He pulled the trigger. Everything went in slow motion. Burt could hear the sound of his own breath and realized that he'd seen this exact scenario play out in his dreams. It was the shot.

The bullet flew over Burt's head. Just as it hit a wine bottle another man entered the saloon and pointed his gun at Jeff. All the patrons scrambled to find safe cover in the saloon.

"Billy? Is that you?" asked Burt.

Burt recognized the gun; it was his own.

Jeff immediately turned and saw Billy Stiles aiming the gun at him. Both men were now in a standoff as Burt watched.

"It doesn't have to end this way," Billy announced.

"Once I'm done with you, your friend is next," said Jeff.

Both men circled one another around a set of pool tables, neither one backing down. Burt felt an object touch his boots and looked down to see a pool cue. He picked it up and held it tight thinking about how he could help Billy. Burt then approached Jeff from behind and hit him hard on the shoulder where he'd been shot.

As he was struck, Jeff fired his weapon at Billy.

In response, Billy shot back. Blood splattered over Burt's shirt as Jeff landed face first across a pool table. Billy then hit the floor landing on his knees holding his stomach. Jeff was instantly killed with the bullet going through his head.

Burt then slid down to help his old friend. "Why did you come here?" Burt asked, holding Billy.

"I don't know, something inside told me to come here," Billy said, his face grew pale. Billy then fell back and Burt broke his fall with his arms. "I am a goner. Please make sure you do something good in your life," said Billy.

"Don't say that. You're going to make it. I'll get you to a doctor," Burt said as a tear ran down his face.

Billy then closed his eyes and faded away into death.

Burt grimaced and slammed his fist on the ground. "Nooo!" Burt yelled hysterically.

Mr. Dubois then popped his face up from behind the bar surveying the scene. He saw Burt sitting there on the floor. "Best leave now if you want any chance at a new life," said Mr. Dubois.

Burt stood with anguish in his eyes but not before grabbing the gun, his gun, from Billy.

"I won't tell anyone the truth about what happened here. Consider this my favor in return to you," said Mr. Dubois.

Burt slowly backed away looking at his friend one last time and ran out the door. He hopped onto what was Jeff Milton's horse and left town heading south toward the farm in Mexico.

It was just him and his thoughts for the next couple of days. He knew he'd dreamed of the event in the saloon multiple times in his life but nothing had prepared him for losing his friend. He had lost everything he ever worked for, and was confident as well that he had lost Kate.

A few days after the event Burt made it back to the farmhouse. Outside, he was greeted by Francisco *No Eyes* Nieves who was glad to see him.

"Long journey?" he asked Burt surveying his dirt-covered face.

"Yes, very long. It is good to see you old friend," said Burt.

"Why don't you come inside, there is someone here who would like to see you," said Nieves.

Burt opened the door and stood frozen as he heard the voice of a female enthusiastically say, "It's about time!"

27: THE WATER

The handle of his shovel was jagged. Splinters littered his hands. Sweat dripped from his brow. Burt took a break from the work and stretched breathing in the humid Panama air. It was October 1906 and the construction of the Panama Canal was well underway led by the United States. Homes, dance halls, theatres, and even a baseball field had been built to entertain the workers. To him, the lifestyle was much better than anything Los Angeles had provided; not to mention the bonds he'd made with the other workers that were people just like him. The now thirty-nine-year-old Burt was well received for his strength and ability to speak English, and quickly was given the job of managing a team of fifty laborers who were working on the Gatun Dam. Though he did not need to, he worked just as hard physically as his men. While the work was strenuous, it kept Burt's mind sane, and he had Kate to go home to.

Though Burt had never played baseball he had been recruited to one of the teams because he was the only person that could throw left-handed. Games were played on their only day off, Sundays. Burt was reluctant to play, however, he played along with the recruiter's request because he'd remembered how his old boss at the O.K. Corral had always dreamed of playing for the Chicago Cubs. Burt played for the Panama Athletic Club who wore caps with an embroidered PAC. Only four teams were in the league, and they played against every team five times during the season, with the best two records playing in the championship. Burt learned the game quickly and his teammates discovered the one thing he was good at, pitching. His raw strength allowed him to throw the ball faster than anyone else in the league. As a result, his team had the best record in the league and coasted into the championship game. Their opponent in the championship game was a team they hated, known as the Stars of the Pacific. Burt of course was the starting pitcher, and what follows is the story of the last inning of that game.

The score was 5 to 4 with the Panama Athletic Club ahead. Burt had pitched the whole game leading into the last inning. The first batter of the game, Bryce Ortega bunted, allowing him to easily get on base. The next batter came up and quickly had two strikes. Burt's hands came together, then looked at the runner on first base. The runner had a short lead so Burt lifted his knee, reached back and hurled the ball forward. Red Lucas was up to bat and watched as the ball left Burt's hands. However, Red was unprepared in timing the pitch like he had for the previous two pitches. Before Red could swing, the ball was in the glove of the catcher.

"Strike three!" yelled the umpire.

The hundreds of people who showed up to the game, mostly consisting of other Canal workers cheered loudly. There was now one out in the inning with a runner on first base. Burt dug his foot into the dirt on the side of the pitching rubber before resting his foot up against it.

Tom Wright approached the plate next. He'd already gotten two hits off Burt during the game. With anticipation of the game soon concluding the spectators' uneasy energy was felt among both teams. Burt's heart was racing though he showed no emotion. His first pitch was a ball, followed by another one. The count was now two ball and no strikes. The catcher signaled a fastball. Burt lifted his knee and threw the ball once more but it flew over the heart of the plate and Tom belted a double in the left center field gap. Bryce made it to third base safely while Tom ran to second base. The crowd could not contain their excitement. Burt then realized the crowd did not care who won, they just enjoyed watching the battle.

If it's drama they want, drama they shall get, Burt thought to himself. He recognized the situation at hand. There was only one out and they were not in a good position to get a double play. Burt called for time-out and waved his catcher over to him.

"I'm going to walk the next guy on purpose," said Burt.

"You're going to do what?" asked the catcher.

"We need a double play, just trust me," explained Burt.

The catcher shook his head as he walked back to home plate.

"Play Ball!" yelled the umpire, and just as Burt had said, he threw four straight balls outside, effectively walking the batter. Burt then called for time-out again, this time calling in all of his infielders.

"Alright boys this guy's a right-handed batter and he's been late on the ball for the whole game. Expect the ball to go to the right. I want my first baseman and third baseman standing closer than usual, in case of a ground ball throw it to the catcher to get the out at home. My shortstop and second baseman play back and get the double play," directed Burt.

His infielders looked at him with an odd expression, each wondering if he'd lost his mind. "Listen to me and go back to your positions please boys," pleaded Burt.

They all shook their heads as they headed to where Burt wanted them positioned. As the infielders ran back, the crowd became louder and louder. Burt scanned the crowd before suddenly stopping and locking eyes with Kate. She gave him a gentle nod letting him know that he had this.

Burt stepped back onto the pitcher's mound, foot up against the rubber; hands came set as the next batter, Joe Brown, waited for the pitch. Burt lifted his knee again and located his fastball toward the outside of the plate. Joe swung hitting a weak ground ball to the second baseman that fielded the ball clean, tossed it to the shortstop covering second base. The crowd screamed, and Joe sprinted down the line knowing that if he could get safe on first the game would be tied. The shortstop caught the ball with his foot on the bag, and then stepped to throw it to first base just as the runner slid into his feet. The ball came out of his hand with a zip before he fell to the ground dramatically. The crowd jumped into the air hoping to get the best view as the ball sailed to the first baseman. The first baseman stretched his arm out as far as he could while still holding his foot on the base. Joe was a step away from the base as the ball entered the glove, a very close play, a call from the umpire could go either way.

"He's out!" yelled the umpire.

The crowd went wild. "What an ending! PAC wins!" the announcer spoke into his microphone. Burt's teammates crowded around him patting him on the back and shaking his hand. Kate came out onto the field and gave him a hug.

The team was presented with a golden team trophy which was first given to Burt. He held it up into the air as the crowd applauded. Burt then handed the trophy to one of his teammates and he and Kate walked off the field. They headed toward their favorite area, a cliff overlooking the Pacific Ocean. The sun was getting close to setting at this point.

"Billy would have enjoyed watching that," Burt said in a sorrowful tone.

"Watched it? Billy would have played in the game," Kate smiled.

Burt agreed and nodded as Kate continued. "You look well rested, more than usual. Are your bad dreams gone?" she asked.

Burt closed his eyes for a moment and took a deep breath before answering. Kate held Burt's hand as they faced the ocean and someone tapped him on the shoulder. Burt turned to see who it was. It was a heavyset man with round glasses, gray mustache, and in a nice clean suit. Burt looked at him like he recognized him but couldn't seem to find the name.

"President Roosevelt! What a surprise," said Kate.

"What a wonderful game. Burt, you pitched magnificently, I saw the whole game," said President Roosevelt.

Burt gulped. He did not know if his past had caught up with him or if Roosevelt truly did not know who he was. "Thank you, Mr. President," said Burt.

"I am here to check on the progress of the Canal. I've heard great things about you working on Gatun Dam. I'd like to offer you more responsibility, are you up for it?" President Roosevelt asked.

Burt stuttered unable to find words. Kate saw the shock in his eyes and slapped him on the back. Burt snapped out of it, "Yes, of course."

"Great, I want you to work under Sydney Williamson who is in charge of the Pacific Division. Take a look over there," President Roosevelt pointed to an area of land touching the Pacific Ocean. "That is where we will make the cut for the water to enter the Canal, and you will help Sydney. When this is all completed, it will change many lives for the better. You see, we must dare to be great; and we must realize that greatness is the fruit of toil and sacrifice and high courage."

"I'm up for the task, you can count on me Mr. President," said Burt.

President Roosevelt patted Burt on the back as Kate held his hand. The three then looked out at the Pacific as the sun began its dive into the ocean. Bright orange and blue colors filled the sky. President Roosevelt stood next Burt who was hugging Kate. Burt then answered Kate's earlier question, "My bad dreams are over."

PHOTOS

Burt Alvord

Billy Stiles   Jeff Milton   Wyatt Earp

George Parsons   Frank McLaury   Big Nose Kate

ACKNOWLEDGMENTS

First, this novel would not exist if it was not for my grandfather's love of our family's history. I have enjoyed every moment writing this and am grateful for the opportunity. Thank you to my mother-in-law, Cristina, for taking the time to help with the editing. Thank you to my wife, Stefanie for your input in the cover design and support.

ABOUT THE AUTHOR

Bobby Brown earned a degree in history at the University of Arizona. He knew that one day he would be a writer. He was also a student-athlete on the baseball team, winning the 2012 College Baseball World Series. Writing was put on hold as he played Minor League Baseball for the Kansas City Royals. Since then, Bobby has been a successful baseball and softball coach. He still had a passion for studying history but found little time to write. When the COVID-19 pandemic began in 2020, Bobby, like many others, was left with a lot of free time. Bobby decided to devote his time to writing, publishing two books, first his baseball autobiography, *Overcoming the Bench – A Baseball Guide to Players, Coaches & Parents*, then a historical fiction novel, *Of Space and Time – The Last Pandemic*. Bobby lives in San Diego with his wife, two daughters, and one dog.